ALL ABOUT...

MUSIC
TECHNOLOGY
IN WORSHIP

By Steve Young

Edited by Corey Fournier

Foreword by Rory Noland

Illustrations by Robby Berman

HAL•LEONARD

Published by Hal Leonard Corporation
7777 Bluemound Road
P.O. Box 13819
Milwaukee, WI 53213

Trade Book Division Editorial Offices
151 West 46th Street, 8th Floor
New York, NY 10036
Library of Congress Cataloging-in-Publication Data:

Young, Steve, 1967-
  All about-- music technology in worship / by Steve Young.-- 1st ed.
     p. cm.
  ISBN 0-634-05449-X (pbk.)
  1. Electronic music--Instruction and study. 2. Church
music--Instruction and study. I. Title.
MT724.Y68 2004
786.7'171--dc22

                              2003025454

Printed in the United States of America
First Edition
Book Designed by Hal Leonard Creative Services

HAL•LEONARD®
Visit Hal Leonard online at
www.halleonard.com

Acknowledgments

I want to thank the team of people without whom this book would not be possible: Corey Fournier, editor extraordinaire and a great friend. Your consistent encouragement and assistance were invaluable in this project! Additional thanks go to Paul Youngblood at Roland U.S.; illustrator Robby Berman; musical partners Dave Owens and Brian Swerdfeger; and Belinda Yong at Hal Leonard.

Additionally, I'm greatly indebted to my friends and family at Renaissance Church for providing me with a *long leash* while tackling this project. It's a privilege to serve with you.

Additional thanks go to my friends and partners in ministry who were willing to share their stories and expertise with me. I'm honored to partner with you in building His Kingdom.

Finally, co-writing credits are deserved for my wife, Victoria, and my two boys, Jordan and Brady. Your patience, encouragement and support have been superhuman and an invaluable part of this project. I love you!

CONTENTS

FOREWORD

by Rory Noland

In the early '80s, I bought a synthesizer. After a few months I knew that instrument inside and out. I learned how to use the breath controller and the modulation wheel, but when I started to customize my patches I was faced with a dilemma. At that point, I realized that I could spend all of my waking hours programming synth patches. In fact, some professional keyboard players I admired were making a living by programming their own custom sounds. The question was not whether this was a good use of someone's time, but whether it was the best use of my time. It wasn't. I'm a music director in a church and like everyone else involved in church work, paid staff or volunteer, ministry keeps me extremely busy. If I locked myself in my office and put all my time into mastering all the intricacies of today's music technology, it would undoubtedly take time away from ministering to the people I've been called to serve. After all, ministry is not just services and programs. Ministry is people. So how does one balance the need for learning the technology with the demands of ministry? That's where this book can be of invaluable help.

Today, music technology continues to play an increasingly important role in church ministry. From electric guitars to synthesizers, from MIDI sequencing to hard disk recording, from drum loops to amplifiers, church music has definitely entered the electronic age. We can't afford to ignore the technical side of ministry anymore. The first challenge, for those of us in church music, is to learn the new technology.

The second challenge involves using the technology in a way that enhances ministry. This book will help you meet both of those challenges.

Steve has a knack for explaining the technical aspects of electronic music in a way that's quickly understood and easy to grasp. If you have no background in technology or if you've been intimidated by it in the past, you will find Steve's approach very easy to follow. Because it's written in laymen's terms, this book will help you understand all you need to know about music technology in the church.

Steve has many years of experience in serving a variety of local churches as a musician, a ministry leader, and a consultant. So whether you're in a large church or a small one, a contemporary setting or one that's traditional, you will find the material covered in this book to be deeply beneficial and highly relevant. Steve's experience in church music has also given him a solid understanding of the purpose of ministry. He is sensitive to the needs of the musicians on the platform as well as the average person sitting out in the congregation. He is not one to lose sight of what's really important in music ministry: loving God and loving people. So even though this is a book about music technology, its author knows that the technology is subservient to the message.

Because many of us musicians in the church have had our lives significantly changed by this message, we have a strong desire to serve the Lord with the talents He's entrusted to us. Out of sheer gratitude for all God has done for us, we want to give something back to Him. David, a musician, felt the same way. He wrote, "What shall I render to the Lord for all His benefits toward me?" (Psalm 116:12). We can give Him the best of our time and talents. This book will enhance your musicianship and allow you to offer the Lord more of your best for His glory.

—Rory Noland

*Rory Noland is music director for Willow Creek Community Church
in South Barrington, Illinois.*

INTRODUCTION
THE TECHNOLOGY GENE

Growing up in a Lutheran pastor's home, I never considered myself a technical person. This was mainly due to my parents' aversion to all things technical—we didn't have a computer, a fancy stereo, or even an answering machine. While we certainly weren't wealthy, it wasn't money that was keeping us out of the technological world as much as it was genetics (more on that later). The truth is that the biggest technological day in the Young household during my youth was the day we got a microwave oven. We didn't mess around when it came to food!

Being raised in such a "technophobic" environment didn't exactly set me up for a career as a contemporary musician. Nevertheless, I saved up enough money to buy my first synthesizer. When I got it home, I figured out how to play the preset sounds, but that was about it. What was this "MIDI" thing? And what about words like "arpeggiator" and "oscillator"? Did I accidentally buy the Italian version? After reading the manual, I was convinced: I *did* buy the Italian version! But that wasn't the worst of it. I had friends with synthesizers who seemed immune to the confusion and frustration that accompanied just about every moment I spent with this instrument for which I'd saved my money for years.

So, why is it that some of us seem to have the innate ability to immediately understand anything with buttons on it, while others run for cover at the sight of a remote control? I'm convinced—though not yet supported by modern science—that there is a technology gene, and I can tell you with complete confidence that some people have it, and some don't. Those who are blessed with this rarest of genes have little use for owner's manuals. They are able to master each new technological innovation in short order. They're not always great musicians; in fact, some are quite ordinary. Nevertheless, they are the object of much envy by those less-fortunate souls who are born without the gene. As a card-carrying member of the technologically challenged, I had to learn about music technology the old-fashioned way: with great determination, perseverance, and countless phone calls to my genetically gifted friends!

Now, before I get bombarded with email challenging my less-than-scientific conclusions, I'll admit it: I made it up! While the notion of a technology gene may indeed be far-fetched, I've discovered that this description of delving into the world of music technology is one that resonates with many church musicians. While, in my own story, I count myself among the technologically challenged, I've since discovered that I am not alone in this struggle. In fact, I've found that the church is full of people like me.

Before you start thinking about returning this book, I should point out that I've come to understand, appreciate, and even embrace technology in my life. I'm living proof that even the technologically challenged can prevail in this area. After finishing school, I began to work as a keyboard player in the Los Angeles area. I learned to understand synthesizers, a then-new technology called "MIDI," and even computers. In fact, this technology paid my rent as I played keyboards in studios as well as with various bands. It wasn't long before I became aware of God's call into full-time ministry, and I accepted my first staff position at a church. While leading the worship ministry of a large Southern California church, we regularly used synthesizers, MIDI sequencing, and various other expressions of music technology to enhance our congregation's worship life. My, how things change!

In the late 1990s, I started a ministry called Arts Impact, which is a giant umbrella under which I do a variety of arts-related ministry projects. However, the main focus of Arts Impact is to partner with local church leaders—providing coaching, mentoring, and instruction in key ministry areas. It wasn't long before I discovered that music technology was a key area of frustration in many churches. As a result,

I've had the opportunity to teach workshops for other organizations such as Maranatha Music, Integrity Music, and the Willow Creek Association, as well as my own Worship Impact workshops. As we have all experienced, technology evolves at a pace that is difficult to keep up with under the best of circumstances. And what about music technology in worship? I'm going to go out on a limb and suggest that change is not something that most of our churches look forward to.

But fear not! There is hope! Music technology in worship is not something to fear, it's something to enjoy. Today's musical tools are accessible to even the most genetically challenged. Synthesizers have greater capabilities than ever, yet are also easier to use. While yesterday's electronic musical instruments were mainly for keyboard players, current music technology includes electronic percussion, guitar synthesizers, bass processors, hard disk recorders, and wind controllers. There are powerful tools now available for churches of all shapes, sizes, and backgrounds.

Currently, music technology is utilized in virtually every worship context imaginable. It wasn't long ago that electronic musical instruments were a luxury that only the largest churches could afford. But now, even the most sophisticated instruments are commonly found in small churches, church "plants," and missions. And while these instruments have long been associated with contemporary musical styles, traditional churches are increasingly finding ways for music technology to enhance their ministries as well. So whether your church sings hymns or choruses, has a band or an organ, is large or small, and no matter the denomination, music technology can open up a whole new world of possibility for your ministry.

How to Use This Book

It is my firm conviction that any open-minded individual who is willing to invest a little effort toward learning music technology will reap huge benefits in their ministry. If you're technologically challenged like me, this book is written for you! Perhaps you're an experienced church musician but haven't yet found a way to include electronic musical instruments into your ministry. Or maybe you've tried to learn music technology but have experienced a level of frustration along the way. Maybe you're a guitarist or percussionist who has long thought that the world of music technology was exclusively for keyboard players. Or perhaps you're already knee-deep in the world of music technology but would like to deepen your knowledge and add a few colors to your creative palette. Wherever you sit on this spectrum, this book is written for you!

As technology continues to evolve and expand, new and exciting tools are becoming available and more affordable almost daily. This makes the scope of a book like this somewhat daunting. As soon as the ink dries, there is likely to be a new innovation that wasn't covered here. So how can we cover such an important subject with any level of accuracy or credibility?

While technology is in a constant state of change, the needs of most church musicians remain consistent. We still need instruments that provide a variety of great sounds. We also need the ability to control or enhance those sounds. We need tools that help us create, arrange, and prepare music. We need tools to help us rehearse, and even tools for recording music. But, perhaps most of all, we need technology that engages people and facilitates worship from the heart. Therefore, this book is designed to help you grow with the technological changes that will inevitably come. Instead of head-in-the-clouds technical theory, you'll learn the real world concepts and applications behind current and future music technology. So when change comes—and it always does—you'll be ready for it. Virtually every application for music technology currently used in the church can be found in these pages. And while individual products may have escaped our radar screen, rest assured that the technology behind those products is fully explored. So before we begin our journey, let's take a look at the major areas of focus found in this book.

Chapter One: A Brief History of Music Technology in Worship
In this chapter, we'll explore the history of electronic musical instruments. We'll open up the world of electronic music to see what is possible in a worship setting. We'll identify the music technology that is most commonly found in today's churches and list the most common applications for these ministry tools.

Chapter Two: The Synthesizer
While the word *synthesizer* has long been synonymous with *keyboards*, this no longer holds true as synthesizers are making their way into the hands of virtually every instrument group. In this chapter, we'll learn the basic terms and concepts behind the synthesizer. Whether you're most comfortable at the keyboard, guitar, drum set, wind instrument, or just sitting at the computer, you'll find the synthesizer demystified in this chapter.

Chapter Three: MIDI Revealed

What exactly is MIDI? What does it do? How can it help me? These and other questions are answered as we discover how MIDI technology works, how MIDI technology is used in a worship setting, and how it can help you in your ministry.

Chapter Four: MIDI Sequencing in a Worship Context

Building on our newfound knowledge of MIDI, we'll dive head first into the world of MIDI sequencing. We'll learn what types of sequencers are available as well as their strengths and weaknesses. We'll discover what a Standard MIDI File is and how it can help your congregation. We'll take a peek at how MIDI sequencing is used in real-life ministry situations and explore how this powerful technology can help you in your worship setting. We'll even take a look at how computer-notation software can be integrated into your church's music ministry. The terms and concepts covered in this chapter will allow you to hit the ground running in virtually any sequencing system.

Chapter Five: Playing Keyboards in Worship

In this section, we embark on a guided tour through the world of keyboards. We'll look at keyboards of various sizes and features. Keyboards with weighted or unweighted keys, synthesizers, digital pianos, workstations, and digital organs are all explored here. We'll discuss how to determine which keyboard is the best fit for your unique worship situation. We'll also distinguish between the various roles that keyboard players are asked to play, how to play them, as well as discover tips to getting the most out of your keyboard setup.

Chapter Six: Guitar Technology in Worship

How can a guitar player utilize music technology to its fullest? In this chapter, we'll examine the various types of guitars commonly found in houses of worship. We'll also explore new sounds that are possible on today's guitars using guitar synthesizers, effects processors, and various amplification technology.

Chapter Seven: Bass Technology in Worship

Building on our knowledge of the guitar, we'll explore music technology options for bass players. Effects processors aren't just for guitar players anymore. In this section, we'll learn about a variety of basses, bass amplifiers, and bass processors. We'll also examine how the role of the bass player relates to electronic music technology.

Chapter Eight: Electronic Percussion in Worship

The electronic drum kit isn't the only option available to churches wishing to include percussion in their worship. In this section, we'll take a tour of the world of electronic percussion instruments. We'll also learn how churches of various backgrounds are successfully adding this element to their services in creative ways.

Chapter Nine: Hard Disk Recording in a Worship Setting

While a hard disk recorder isn't a musical instrument per se, churches of all traditions and sizes are using this exciting new technology to enhance their ministries. Whether it's creating CDs from the pastor's sermon or producing a full-length worship recording, we'll unpack this growing area of technology. We'll cover hardware- and software-recording solutions with special emphasis on ministry applications.

Chapter Ten: Music Technology in a Small Church Setting

It wasn't long ago when high-tech tools were only available to large churches with gargantuan budgets. But today's tools are more accessible than ever to small and new churches. In this chapter, we'll discover some tips for making *big* music in a small church setting. We'll also encounter several real-life examples of churches who benefit regularly from these powerful tools.

Chapter Eleven: Music Technology in a Traditional Church Setting

Are churches with traditional worship limited to the pipe organ? Not anymore. In this chapter, we'll discover that *singing a new song* doesn't have to involve straying from the time-honored. We'll learn how to enhance the traditional worship service with modern technology in a way that embraces your church's worship heritage.

Chapter Twelve: Advanced Applications for Music Technology in Worship

While this book is not written to an advanced audience, there will undoubtedly be those who are curious as to what the cutting edge has to offer in their church. In this section we'll explore the world of possibility as we profile several ways that churches are pushing the envelope of creativity in worship through music technology.

Chapter Thirteen: Purchasing Equipment for Your Organization

In the ever-changing world of music technology, it is highly likely that your church is either considering a purchase in the next 12 months or has recently made such a purchase. Because this process is second only to the reading of the manual in terms of potential frustration, it is important that we include it in our discussion. We'll learn how to choose wisely, putting good stewardship principles to work during the entire process of purchasing equipment for your ministry.

Chapter Fourteen: Keeping the Main Thing, the Main Thing

In a world of technology, it's easy to forget why the technology is here in the first place. In this chapter we'll wrestle with merging ministry values and the use of technology in worship.

Appendix: Next Steps

Now that we've gained a greater understanding of what music technology can bring to worship, how can we continue to learn and grow as technology evolves? We'll look at some great resources that can help facilitate continued growth, equipping and empowering you to reap the benefits of music technology in worship.

To assist in navigating the vast waters of music technology, you'll encounter several visual *icons* that are designed to help contextualize what you are reading. Here is a breakdown of each icon:

 History: When you encounter the *history* icon, you'll read about the origins of a particular area of music technology. You'll also discover how that technology has evolved over time and how it is used today—particularly in a ministry context.

 Nuts and Bolts: This is where you'll learn all the *nuts and bolts* of how music technology works. When you see this symbol, you'll find a full explanation of a given area of music technology.

 Ministry Snapshots: This book is all about real-life application. Therefore, in each chapter you'll find *ministry snapshots*. These are brief profiles of real people in real ministry situations who are using music technology in powerful ways. Through reading their stories, you'll be inspired and empowered to utilize music technology in amazing ways.

 Lifesavers: When you encounter the *lifesaver* symbol, you'll learn specific application tips, such as common uses of a particular technology, time-saving tips, and tricks that the pros use. The common bond that these *lifesavers* share is that they will make life easier and ensure that music technology in worship is more about *worship* than *technology*.

As you can see, there's a lot of information packed into these pages. And while you may find an area or two that isn't covered, I believe you'll find everything you need to get started in a powerful way. While some readers will be tempted to skip ahead to the chapter that contains their instrument, I'd encourage each of you to take the opportunity to learn about the other instruments you'll be serving with and their players. Not only will it help you understand their mind-set, but it will help you become a better player, as you'll develop a better grasp of how your own part fits in with the other instruments. For church leaders, developing a working under-standing of the various instruments commonly used in worship is the first step to better arranging skills and more fluid and efficient rehearsals. It is my hope that we all overcome our technical reluctance in order to unleash the creativity that God intended in our congregations and communities.

ONE

A BRIEF HISTORY OF MUSIC TECHNOLOGY IN WORSHIP

Before we explore today's electronic musical instruments, it's helpful to look at the past. Traditional churches like to speak of their worship *heritage*. Indeed, looking at the past can help us better understand the present as well as the future. Therefore, we're going to look at the *heritage* of music technology in worship and how that heritage has shaped the technology of today.

Diversity in the area of musical instruments utilized in worship is not a new concept. The Old Testament states that "David and all the Israelites were celebrating with all their might before God, with songs and with harps, lyres, tambourines, cymbals, and trumpets" (1 Chron. 13:8). By this account, stringed, percussive, and wind instruments were already in use in a worship context over 3,000 years ago. Yet, after the development of the pipe organ, few new instruments found their way into houses of worship—that is, until the twentieth century.

In 1919 a Russian inventor named Leon Theremin created the first fully electronic musical instrument, which bears his name. Largely experimental in nature, the Theremin is played by waving one's hands in the vicinity of two antennae. One controls pitch, and the other controls volume. The sound of a Theremin is often equated with the high-pitched, eerie sound heard in many sci-fi films of the 1950s, and also in pop music of the 1960s.

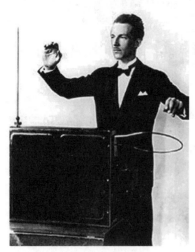

Leon Theremin

In 1927, a headline in the *Toronto Star* newspaper read, "Young Canadian Invents Pipeless Ethereal Organ." In 1928, Morse Robb, the young inventor from Belleville, Ontario, filed the first patent for an electric organ. Although he beat Laurens Hammond to the punch (Hammond filed his patent in 1934), the Robb Wave Organ didn't hit the market until 1936. By 1941 only thirteen Robb Wave Organs had been sold.

In 1945, another Canadian, Hugh Le Caine, developed the Electronic Sackbut, an instrument that became known as the world's first voltage-controlled synthesizer. Robert Moog, a Cornell trained physicist who was fascinated by the Theremin, unveiled his famous modular synthesizer in 1965. Others followed Moog's example in creating new and exciting electronic instruments. What Theremin, Robb, and Hammond began, and Le Caine, Moog, and others refined, has blossomed into a whole world of musical possibility that continues today.

Churches, playing the surprising role of early adopter, began to utilize electric organs in the 1950s. By the 1970s, with the dawn of the contemporary worship movement, synthesizers were beginning to appear in houses of worship. Though the electric guitar pickup was first patented by the Gibson Guitar Company in 1937, it was more than 30 years later when churches began to put electric guitars to use.

Moog Modular Synthesizer

Roland System 700 Synthesizer

The advent of the personal computer in the 1980s was a huge milestone in the world of music technology. Synthesizers that were once controlled by electric voltage began using digital microchip technology. This technology allowed real acoustic instruments to be digitally recorded, or *sampled*, and reproduced with amazing realism by keyboards, drum pads, guitars, and even wind instruments. The lines between traditional instruments and synthesizers continued to blur as technology that was formerly available only to keyboardists became accessible to guitarists and other instrumentalists. In 1983 MIDI was born. This new technology allowed musicians to network their instruments, allowing unprecedented sound and flexibility. It also allowed musical instruments to be connected to computers, which has forever changed the landscape of music composition, printing, and recording.

Through this incredible technological revolution, churches have done their best to keep pace, albeit cautiously. With one eye on the traditions of the past and one eye on the emerging generations of new parishioners, church musicians have focused mainly on ways to emulate those instruments that are familiar to its members: the pipe organ, the piano, and various orchestral instruments. But, in recent years, a new generation of church musicians, many raised in the age of the personal computer, have sought to bring exciting new instruments, sounds, and technology into the worship experience.

While it's taken a largely youthful push to bring this technology into the church, even traditionally minded churches are finding that electronic musical instruments can enhance the *tried and true* as well as the *new*.

In today's churches, musicians are using synthesizers to recreate majestic pipe organs, world-class grand pianos, and entire string sections. But they're also using digital signal-processing technology to enhance the sound of acoustic and electric guitars, bass guitars, voices, and other instruments.

A desktop MIDI studio

Percussionists, both traditional and contemporary, are finding that electronic music technology allows them access to a world of exotic instruments with a minimum of physical space and budget, not to mention easy transport. Small churches are augmenting their modest musical resources with pre-programmed *MIDI sequences* or recordings that essentially give them the same capabilities as churches with large ensembles. Musical scores for choirs, soloists, orchestras, congregations, and praise bands are being created on personal computers with powerful and inexpensive software. Many congregations are even creating high-quality, in-house worship recordings, using affordable and portable hard disk recording technology without the expense of renting a professional recording studio.

While we've experienced some incredible highlights in the last 100 years, the future looks brighter than ever as new innovations in music technology are now a common occurrence. As computer processing gets faster and more powerful, technology that is unthinkable today is likely to be readily available and affordable in the coming years. The church is indeed poised to carry the torch of musical diversity that David modeled for us in I Chronicles. Is it any surprise that David wrote in Psalm 33:3, "Sing to him a new song. Play skillfully and shout for joy"?

TWO

THE SYNTHESIZER

When Leon Theremin first played his new musical invention for Lenin, he scarcely could have known the chain reaction that was to follow. His strange, new instrument was as controversial as it was rare and mysterious. Over eighty years later, what began as extraordinary has become quite commonplace. Today, synthesizers have become staples in houses of worship. And, although the technology continues to evolve, there are concepts and terms that virtually all synthesizers share. This chapter is designed to provide an overview of the modern synthesizer, as well as to provide real-world tools that will enable you to better utilize the synthesizer in a worship setting. Look for the various helper icons that are included along the way.

As we discovered in Chapter One, the synthesizer was first introduced in 1945 by Canadian inventor Hugh Le Caine. The very first synthesizers were based on

A classic analog monophonic synthesizer

the concept of *control voltage*. Higher voltages created higher sounds while lower voltages resulted in lower sounds. These large, clumsy instruments were *monophonic*—that is, they were only capable of playing one note at a time. To create different sounds, short electrical cables (called patch cables) were used to feed the control voltage to various components within the instruments. Special organ-like keyboards were built to allow pianists or organists to play the instrument. These early synthesizers with cables hanging everywhere were similar in appearance to an old switchboard, where the operator would have to connect two callers using a patch cable.

The Yamaha WX-5 MIDI wind controller in action

Although control-voltage synthesizers (also called analog synthesizers) have largely been replaced by digital synthesizers, analog and digital technology share a common heritage. As a result, some of the concepts and terms associated with today's most advanced electronic musical instruments haven't changed since the days of the big dinosaur synthesizers. Even so, synthesizers have evolved at the same breakneck pace that we're used to seeing in all areas of technology. Consequently, there have been amazing new additions (and subtractions) to the modern synthesizer.

Nowadays, access to synthesizers is not limited to keyboard players. Today's synthesizers are available to guitarists, bassists, percussionists, and those who play wind instruments. Some *synths* have piano- or organ-type keyboards, others are simply *boxes* with a few buttons on the front, and yet others have no shape at all—they're simply software running on a computer (software synthesizers). And while the motto seems to be "no boundaries," today's synthesizers still share the same family tree. Most, if not all, of these new types of synthesizers are making their way into houses of worship. After all, they are powerful instruments with great potential to create moving music. But don't let the scope of these instruments scare you. It is possible to understand what makes these things tick. What follows are some terms and concepts that virtually all synthesizers share.

Sampling Technology

Until the 1980s, the only synthesizers available were *analog* (control voltage) synthesizers. The part of the analog synthesizer that actually created the sound was called a *voltage control oscillator* or *VCO*. The VCO was capable of producing a few different kinds of simple sounds. These sounds are identified by the shape of their waveforms (square, sawtooth, triangle, etc.). Various filtering techniques were employed to further refine the sound. While this type of synthesis can yield some amazing results, the sense of realism was missing when trying to emulate familiar acoustic instruments like piano or strings.

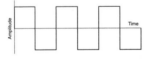

Square waveform

Sawtooth waveform

Triangle waveform

Originally shown in 1979, an instrument called the *Fairlight CMI* (Computer Music Instrument) changed everything. The Fairlight, which originally cost over $25,000, used a new technology called *digital sampling* to create its sounds. This involved recording an acoustic source, such as a piano, digitizing the sound, and storing it in the synthesizer's memory. A keyboardist could then trigger this sound by playing a key on the keyboard. Though the Fairlight was primitive by today's standards, it set a new benchmark in terms of realism. When it was played, no longer would you hear an awkward, analog imitation of an acoustic sound. Rather, you'd now hear

The Fairlight CMI

an *actual recording* of the original acoustic instrument! More than 20 years later, digital-sampling technology is still the basis of most modern synthesizers. However, as you might imagine, a great deal of refinement and improvement to the technology has taken place since the days of the $25,000 Fairlight. In fact, current synthesizers employing digital sampling technology are vastly superior to the original Fairlight and cost about a tenth of the price! Today's sample-based synthesizers contain samples that were recorded using world-class instruments, with the very best microphones, in some of the world's best recording studios. It's like having a $100,000 grand piano at your fingertips one minute, and with the push of a button, you're now playing an eighty-piece orchestra. The possibilities are endless.

Most synthesizers available today contain digital samples of acoustic instruments, such as acoustic piano, pipe organ, and even a string section. Using familiar instruments such as these can help traditional congregations bridge the gap between old and new technologies, allowing synthesizers to be brought into the worship service with a minimum of disruption.

The vast majority of synthesizers made today are *digital* rather than *analog*. Yet it is not uncommon to find a digital synthesizer that contains samples of classic analog synthesizers. This is truly the best of both worlds.

It's important to note that the digital synthesizers we've discussed so far, are those which contain a finite library of sampled sounds. Another type of digital synthesizer, called a *sampler*, allows you to record your own samples and access an infinite variety of commercial sample libraries. While samplers are indeed powerful instruments, their use in the church isn't as common because many synthesizers already have high-quality samples onboard from the manufacturer. However, many of today's synthesizers also have sampling capabilities, offering limitless sonic potential and many useful applications for worship—like using "loops" as we'll discuss in Chapter 12.

Polyphony

In the days of the analog *control-voltage* synthesizers, different kinds of sounds were created by connecting the various components of the synthesizer with patch cables. This made it difficult to switch between different sounds in the best of circumstances, as it usually took several minutes to do so. On top of that, these instruments—from companies like Moog, ARP, Roland, and Sequential Circuits—were *monophonic*; that is, they were only capable of playing a single note at a time, like a wind instrument. So if you wanted to play

Keith Emerson

more than one note at a time and use a variety of sounds in a performance setting, it would only be possible if you had several synthesizers. You may remember seeing rock keyboardists like Rick Wakeman of Yes or Keith Emerson of Emerson, Lake & Palmer standing high on a stage platform that contained over a dozen keyboards. In the early days of synthesizers, this was absolutely necessary in order to have different sounds readily accessible in a performance situation.

Perhaps the most significant early development in the synthesizer was the introduction of the first commercially available *polyphonic* synthesizer by Oberheim. *Polyphony* is simply defined as the ability to play more than one note at a time, like on a piano or an organ. The first *polyphonic* synthesizers were able to play four notes at a time, which was a huge improvement over the previous *monophonic* (single-note) synthesizers. It wasn't long before this number increased to six, then to eight, then to a whopping sixteen and beyond. Today, many synthesizers are able to achieve 128-note polyphony with the potential to go even higher.

 You can help prevent polyphony problems by avoiding the overuse of the sustain pedal and by avoiding playing octaves in the left hand when possible.

Those of us who are pianists are not used to the idea of limits when it comes to the number of notes we can play. Although our fingers can only play ten notes at once, we're accustomed to being able to extend this with the use of the *sustain pedal.* In fact, with the use of "elbow chords" we can play as many notes as we wish (depending on the size of said elbows, of course). You might say that an acoustic piano has 88-note polyphony. Who would need more than this? Actually the answer might surprise you. We'll further explore this concept later in this chapter.

Memory

Another "key" advancement in early synthesizer technology was the development of programmable *memory.* This was the addition of a tiny computer that kept track of the settings of the synthesizer's various knobs and buttons. These settings could then be stored into the synthesizer's memory and be recalled with the push of a single button. This allowed a performer to use only a few, or even a single, keyboard in a performance situation. (I'm sure Rick Wakeman and Keith Emerson's roadies were very happy at this new advancement!) Plus, you could throw away the legal pad where you wrote down all the knob settings on your synth so you could recreate your sounds! Nowadays it's not uncommon to find synthesizers that can hold over one thousand sounds in its onboard memory. The memory capacity of some synthesizers can even be expanded further through the use of various memory cards and disks, resulting in extensive libraries of sounds— all accessible with the touch of a button. It's even possible to store additional sounds on a personal computer through the use of special MIDI software called a *librarian* program.

Tones and Patches

On a modern, sample-based synthesizer, the lowest common denominator of a sound is called a *tone.* A tone is the basic *waveform* that determines the tonal character of a sound. Think of a tone like one of the basic ingredients in a favorite food recipe. The single ingredient (like flour or garlic) may not be much on its own, but when combined with the other ingredients, it's pure heaven! A single tone is rarely heard on its own. Rather, tones are usually combined to create the sounds that we hear when listening to a synthesizer.

For example, a group of tones might be combined to simulate the sound of a guitar. In this example, one tone might be dedicated to creating the "plucking" sound of the string while another tone might be dedicated to creating the round sound of a string that is resonating. Neither tone would sound like a guitar unless they were combined. While this all sounds complicated (and it can be), the good news is that modern synthesizers are programmed at the factory with all sorts of great sounds that give you lots of choices without having to program your own. It's like a buffet!

The combination of tones that create a sound is called a *patch*. The name is reminiscent of the patch cables that were used to create sounds on early analog synthesizers. When we hear the sound of a violin on a modern synthesizer, we are listening to a set of tones combined (like our guitar example) to create a patch. It is common to refer to this as a "violin patch" as opposed to a "violin sound." Therefore, patch is a term used to describe the character or identity of a set of tones.

At first glance, it may seem unnecessary to pay much attention to tones. After all, if tones are part of a patch, then all one really needs to learn in order to use a synthesizer is the concept of patches. This might be true if not for *polyphony*. While our ears typically hear a set of tones as a single patch, or sound, the synthesizer's internal computer sees each tone as a separate note, which, in turn, uses up a note of polyphony. In other words, a patch comprised of four tones may only create one discernable note when middle-C is played on the keyboard, but in this case, it is actually using four notes of polyphony. In the '70s and most of the '80s, when polyphony was well under sixteen notes, this was a huge problem. But because most current synthesizers have at least 64-note polyphony, this is less of a problem. A 128-note synthesizer playing a four-tone patch would allow us to play up to thirty-two keys at the same time. While this seems like more polyphony than we'd ever need, there is one more factor to consider: the sustain pedal.

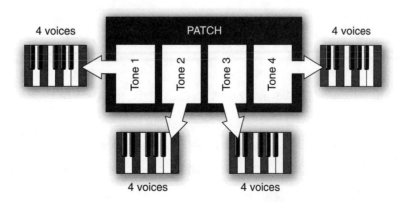

A synthesizer's sustain pedal (often called a *hold* pedal) works differently than the sustain pedal on an acoustic piano. While a piano's sustain pedal is mechanical in nature, the hold function on a synthesizer is an electronic way of holding the notes you've just played. As a result, every note held by the sustain pedal is using up polyphony. Suddenly, the 16-note polyphony found on many synthesizers from the '80s doesn't seem so generous. For those who like to play thick chords with a generous helping of sustain, you'll want a synthesizer with as much polyphony as possible.

Velocity

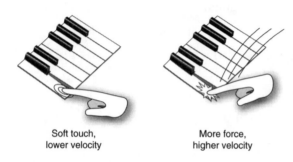

Soft touch,
lower velocity

More force,
higher velocity

Often misunderstood, this term does not refer to the aerodynamic properties of your synthesizer as it's thrown from the window of your office. Rather, it has to do with how the synthesizer responds to dynamic changes in a musician's performance. As musicians, we think of dynamics as varying degrees of loud and soft. The term *velocity*, as it applies to a synthesizer, means that dynamics are measured in terms of the speed at which a key is pressed. While some refer to this as *touch sensitivity*, it is not really *touch* that is measured, but, rather the *velocity* at which the key travels from its uppermost point to its lowermost point. The faster the velocity, the louder the note will sound. The slower the velocity, the softer the note will sound. While this concept may sound a bit odd, try playing some notes on a velocity-sensitive synthesizer and you'll realize that it actually works quite well. While early synthesizers did not have this capability, virtually all synthesizers available today are velocity sensitive.

Layers

We've already learned how a patch is a set of tones combined to create a sound. In a sense, these tones are *layered* to create a patch. However, it's also possible to stack patches on top of each other so that when a note is played, two or more patches sound. This is called *layering*. One of the most common examples of layering in a worship setting is combining a *piano patch* with an *orchestral-string patch*. This allows the keyboardist to create a much bigger and richer sound than a single pianist or string player can create. Because early synthesizers were short on polyphony, the concept of layering was impractical. The only way to layer sounds in those days was to physically play two different synthesizers—one for each hand. Obviously, this would limit what the player could do musically.

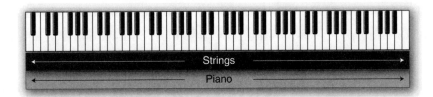

Once MIDI was introduced, two or more synthesizers could be layered together. By connecting synthesizers with MIDI cables, a keyboardist could control several synthesizers from one keyboard. MIDI took layering to the next level, but you still had to have multiple synthesizers.

Today, layering is a common feature found in most synthesizers. Many synthesizers can layer as many as 16 patches internally. It's important to realize, however, that layering two or more patches expends polyphony very, very quickly. While most synthesizers give players the ability to create their own layers, there is usually a good selection of layers included with the synthesizer's factory presets. The ability of a synthesizer to generate more than one instrument, or patch, at a time, is described by the term *multitimbral*. We'll learn more about how multitimbral synthesizers are used in the next few chapters.

Splits

Besides layering, another way that multiple patches are utilized at the same time is called a *split*. A split refers to a synthesizer's ability to assign patches to specific notes. In other words, it's possible to assign one patch to all notes below middle-C while another patch is assigned to the notes above middle-C. Many synthesizers allow for several splits to be used at once—some allow up to 16 patches to be split at once.

A common use of a split on a keyboard is to assign a string bass or a bass guitar sound to notes that would be played by the left hand while assigning a piano patch to notes played by the right hand. The result is the ability for a single keyboardist to sound like two separate instrumentalists. Also, remember that because we're using two or more patches, splits are only possible on multitimbral synthesizers.

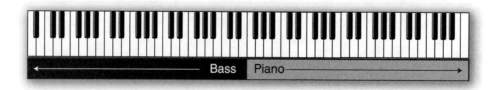

Bass Piano

 Small churches or small ministry settings can benefit from using layers and splits. For example, a church with an acoustic piano and a synthesizer can benefit from music that sounds bigger than one might imagine two musicians can create. Have the synthesizer player use a split that places a string bass patch in the left hand and a string ensemble patch in the right hand. This creates the sound equivalent of several musicians!

Editing

Many synthesizers allow you to customize the sounds and create your own unique patches, layers, and splits. This is in addition to the onboard sounds, also called factory presets. You can alter these sounds to your liking and save them in the synthesizer's internal memory bank, on a memory card, or a floppy disk for easy access. This ability to manipulate sound is called *editing*.

Modulation

The term *modulation* is essentially a technical word that means change. A variety of tonal characteristics on a patch can be changed in real-time. For example, a violinist will add vibrato to a note as it's being held. But that vibrato is not constant throughout the duration of that note. *Modulation* allows a musician to change a characteristic of a patch over time—in this case, adding increasing amounts of vibrato after the note is first played. *Modulation* can be employed using a *modulation wheel* or *lever* on a synthesizer, a foot pedal, or even a beam of light called a D-Beam™.

The D-Beam™, found on many Roland instruments, is a *real-time controller* that allows the user to manipulate or trigger sounds by moving the hand above the D-Beam infrared light.

The D-Beam

The D-Beam in action

Pitch Bend

Unlike some of the other terms we've introduced, *pitch bend* is pretty much what it sounds like: the ability to manually control pitch. Some instruments, like the piano, are fixed-pitch instruments and can only play the notes they were tuned to play. Other instruments, like woodwind or stringed instruments, have the ability to play pitches between half steps. And while you may wonder why anyone would want to do this, consider the opening clarinet solo in Gershwin's "Rhapsody in Blue" or the sound of a gospel singer singing an a capella version of "Amazing Grace." These examples just wouldn't be the same without the ability to *play in the cracks*! Since the early days, synthesizers have had the capability to manually control pitch. About the only thing that's changed is the variety of mechanisms used to do it. The most common pitch benders are wheels and levers. Early synthesizers, and lately some new ones, also utilize a *ribbon controller*. Here, the musician's finger moves along a ribbon strip that manipulates the pitch up or down. New twists on the pitch bender today include the D-Beam™, foot pedals, and aftertouch (pressure applied to a key after it has been struck).

Pitch bend lever

A pitch bend lever is a real-time controller that allows the player to alter the pitch of a note. Many pitch bend levers also allow the user to add modulation to the patch. You can bend the pitch up or down by moving the lever right or left. Modulation is added by pushing the lever forward.

Synth/Sound Modules

The Roland XV-2020 sound module can be played from any MIDI controller

We've established that today's synthesizers are essentially dedicated musical computers that are capable of amazing things. With the introduction of *MIDI technology* (covered in the next chapter), it is now possible to play a synthesizer without actually touching it. Think of changing the channel on your television while using the remote control. You didn't actually touch the television, but you were able to operate it nonetheless. MIDI technology allows the user to operate a synthesizer in a similar manner. Because a synthesizer can be played or controlled without actually being touched, it doesn't have to have its own keyboard. So think of a *sound module* as a synthesizer without the keyboard. While this may be a confusing concept at first, just put it on the back burner for now. We'll unpack it in greater detail in the next chapter.

Other Non-keyboard Instruments

Synthesizers have long been associated with keyboard instruments, and for many years that was the norm. However, in recent years some amazing new non-keyboard synthesizers have made their way into houses of worship. The three most common non-keyboard synthesizers found in worship settings today are:

- Guitar Synthesizers
- Electronic Percussion
- Wind-controller Synthesizers

These synthesizers share the same technology as keyboard synthesizers—they're just played differently. A guitar synthesizer, for example, can access all of the same sounds a keyboard synthesizer can. It is velocity sensitive. It can utilize layers and splits. It can use modulation and pitch bending. The difference is that all of these features are accessed from a *real guitar*! When the guitarist plays a string or a chord, the corresponding notes are triggered in the synthesizer. The sound created can be virtually anything—even a piano or percussion sounds!

An electronic drum kit can sound not only like an acoustic drum kit, but it can also be a set of timpani, a bass guitar, or even a pipe organ! Those who play wind instruments have a whole new world available to them as well. Not only are wind players able to access virtually any kind of sound, but wind controllers allow the player to create modulation or pitch bend using techniques common to wind instrumentalists.

The Roland V-Drums electronic drum kit

***

The synthesizer has indeed changed since the early days. Gone is the necessity to have dozens of instruments for a single performance. The hours needed to connect patch cables and turn knobs to their proper settings have been replaced by a single push of a button. And while yesterday's instruments struggled to emulate familiar acoustic instruments, today's synthesizers can fool even the most discriminating ears. Never before has such powerful technology been so affordable and easy to use. But this is just the beginning.

THREE

MIDI
REVEALED

We learned in Chapter Two that the most significant development in the infancy of the synthesizer was the introduction of *polyphonic* (capable of playing more than one note at a time) synthesizers. Surely the most important development in the synthesizer's adolescent years was the introduction of MIDI technology. Over the last 20 years or so, MIDI technology has redefined how musicians create. MIDI sparked a renaissance, which has reached into every style of music, budget, and venue with a plethora of new tools and the ability to connect them together. In this chapter, we'll demystify this remarkable technology in order to explore what role MIDI might play in your ministry.

It's important to point out that this chapter is one of the most technical in this book. So if you're technologically challenged, you may want to proceed slowly. But your reward will be great if you stick with it. Here's a taste of what you'll be able to accomplish:

- Configure and connect MIDI instruments
- Create rich layers of sounds by connecting MIDI instruments
- Get around the polyphony limitations of synthesizers
- Extend the life of your MIDI instruments
- Expand your ministry using MIDI technology

So what exactly is MIDI? Perhaps the best way to begin is to define what MIDI *is not.* MIDI is not an object. It's not a piece of equipment that you buy in a music store. If you enter your local music store asking, "Where do you keep the MIDIs?" you will immediately identify yourself as a MIDI *rookie.* But don't worry—you won't be one for long. By the end of this chapter you'll be ready to tap into a wonderful area of music technology—one that delivers on its promise to open up a whole new world of creativity to you. So what is MIDI? And what's all the fuss about? As to the former question, MIDI is an acronym. It stands for Musical Instrument Digital Interface. As to what all the fuss is about, read on.

By 1980, computer scientists were implementing powerful and increasingly inexpensive ways to *network* computers. While the power of one computer was amazing enough, two computers working together held even more potential for providing practical solutions for everyday problems. The makers of synthe-

The Roland JX-3P and the Sequential Circuits Prophet 600 connected via MIDI, circa 1983

sizers were well aware of these advancements and envisioned a way for synthesizers to communicate and even collaborate with one another. After all, a synthesizer is essentially a computer. The problem was that each manufacturer had its own idea on how to do this, which meant that you could only connect synthesizers made by the same company. So the call went out to create a standard of communication that allowed electronic music devices of various makes and models to communicate seamlessly. In 1982 this standard was unveiled as the acronym MIDI: Musical Instrument Digital Interface. In 1983 the world's first MIDI synthesizers were introduced by two companies: Roland and Sequential Circuits.

So, we've established that MIDI is a *communication standard* similar to technology that allows computers to communicate through a network. Now, let's break down the components of the MIDI acronym.

The terms *Musical* and *Instrument* imply that MIDI has something to do with musical instruments. That's easy enough—let's look further.

Digital. Well, that's a word we hear most every day, and yet most of us pay no mind to what this word entails. In the early 1980s, digital technology was still new and somewhat mysterious to the average person. But today we live in a *digital world*! The same binary code of 0s and 1s that enables us to listen to CDs, watch DVDs, talk on cordless phones, surf the Internet, organize our lives with a PDA, and watch TV on a satellite network is what comprises the *Digital* in Musical Instrument Digital Interface. It's just a language with a small alphabet: 0 and 1.

But what about *Interface*? An interface, in its most basic form, allows two entities (people, devices, etc.) to communicate or share information. A telephone is a great example of an interface. It facilitates the communication between two—or more—people. Your computer's monitor and mouse are also examples of interfaces. Whether we know it or not, we all use interfaces in our everyday lives.

So, now we know that MIDI is a *standard of digital communication that allows musical instruments to share information.* What's all the fuss about? Consider the following:

- MIDI technology provides *extra hands*, and through layering and MIDI sequencing it allows one musician to create an entire symphony of sound.

- MIDI technology has harnessed the power of the personal computer for musicians, allowing for high-quality and inexpensive solutions for composition, creating printed music, and even audio recording.

- MIDI allows different families of musical instruments, such as keyboards, percussion, guitars, or wind instruments, to communicate and collaborate with each other in new and exciting ways.

Those are just a few of the amazing possibilities MIDI offers. But perhaps the most exciting feature of MIDI is that it is an *open standard*—that is, it can evolve and grow as new technology becomes available. This explains why MIDI technology is more powerful today than it was when introduced over twenty years ago! Let's continue to demystify MIDI through learning some of the basic terms and concepts associated with it.

Audio vs. MIDI

The first thing to understand about MIDI is that it is *not* sound. Remember, MIDI is a system of communicating digital messages—*not analog sound or audio.* Every MIDI-capable synthesizer has MIDI *ports* that facilitate MIDI communication between devices through the use of MIDI cables (more on these later). These MIDI ports can-

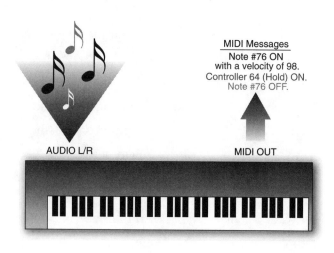

MIDI Messages
Note #76 ON
with a velocity of 98.
Controller 64 (Hold) ON.
Note #76 OFF.

AUDIO L/R   MIDI OUT

Audio vs. MIDI

not be connected to the inputs of a sound system because they carry no sound at all. You can't listen to MIDI through headphones. MIDI has no sound. This cannot be overstated. Many of the misunderstandings that occur when musicians first encounter MIDI technology stem from confusion on this issue. So for the last time (I promise): *MIDI is not sound, nor does it carry sound, replace sound, or substitute for audio cables!*

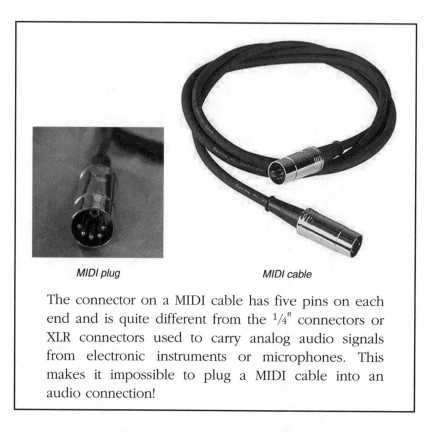

MIDI plug   *MIDI cable*

The connector on a MIDI cable has five pins on each end and is quite different from the ¼" connectors or XLR connectors used to carry analog audio signals from electronic instruments or microphones. This makes it impossible to plug a MIDI cable into an audio connection!

MIDI Messages

So why would we want synthesizers to communicate? And just what is it that we're trying to accomplish? We'll discuss the *"how to"* of connecting MIDI devices shortly. But, for now, let's focus on *what* is being communicated. The earliest, and most common application for connecting MIDI devices is connecting two synthesizers. When two synthesizers are connected, typically one acts as a *master*, or *controller*, and provides the other synthesizer (called a *slave*) with a set of instructions. These instructions are called *MIDI messages*. This is a generic term that describes a variety of specific messages sent between the two devices. We'll focus on the most common messages here.

Note On/Off

The most common MIDI message is called *Note On*. This message is sent when a note is played on the synthesizer that is functioning as the master or controller. The Note On message is sent through a MIDI cable from the master synthesizer to the slave. Now here's where the magic begins: Upon receiving the Note On message from the master, the slave synthesizer automatically plays the same note without being touched by the musician. It's like remote control for musical devices! When the musician stops playing the note, another MIDI message is sent to turn the note off, and as you might guess, the slave synthesizer ceases playing the note automatically.

Specific Note Information

Included in the Note On MIDI message is information identifying the specific note to be played. This information is called the *note number*, or *key number*, and ensures that the slave device will play the proper note when the message is received. Middle-C, for example, is note number 64.

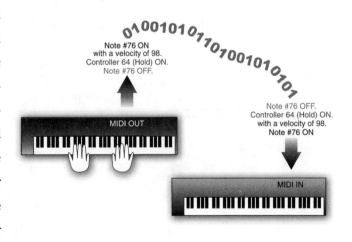

It's important to know that MIDI devices do not share the same range limitations as acoustic instruments. There are a total of 128 (0-127) MIDI note numbers, which is a range greater than a grand piano, which has 88 keys.

::::::::Velocity

You'll recall that we learned in Chapter Two that velocity is used to measure the dynamic level of a musician's performance on a synthesizer. The Note On message also contains velocity information, which is included with the note number as it's sent from the master. So when a note is played on the master synthesizer, the slave synthesizer plays that same note, with the same duration and the same level of velocity. The slave synthesizer accurately imitates the performance on the master. Velocity, like all MIDI messages, is expressed as a value between 0 and 127. Zero is no velocity (the note will not sound), while 127 is maximum. A MIDI instrument will respond in a very musical way as it is played because the dynamics are discrete. For example, three different notes played simultaneously are likely to have three different levels of velocity, which is a reflection of the subtleties of the musician's performance.

Velocity Switching is the ability to trigger different tones or patches by playing a note at varying velocities. This makes it possible for synthesizers to emulate acoustic instruments, which are capable of creating notes with different *timbres*, or character. For example, a guitar can be finger-picked or strummed, creating very different sounds. To emulate this expressiveness, a synthesizer can be programmed to trigger a digital sample (tone) of a finger-picked guitar when played lightly, but trigger a strummed guitar sample when played heavily. The tones are essentially *switched* depending on the velocity with which they are played. While this is probably not something a beginner would want to tackle, the good news is that most synthesizers come with a fair number of velocity switched sounds preinstalled in memory.

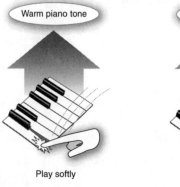

Warm piano tone

Play softly

Bright piano tone

Play harder

Aftertouch

Beyond velocity sensitivity, many MIDI instruments are capable of producing a special controller message called *aftertouch*. Aftertouch provides another level of expressiveness that cannot be created on traditional keyboard instruments. By measuring *key pressure*, it gives the player the ability to change various aspects of the sound *after* a key has been *touched*. If you play and hold a chord on a MIDI keyboard with aftertouch, you can then push on those held keys and create any number of effects, such as a volume swell, a brighter tone, the addition of another sound, vibrato and so on. For example, after playing a chord on a simple piano patch, you could push down gradually for a swell of strings or a thick pad.

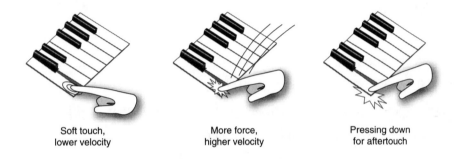

Soft touch,
lower velocity

More force,
higher velocity

Pressing down
for aftertouch

Sustain

Similar to a sustain pedal on a piano, there is a MIDI message called *sustain* that allows a note to be held indefinitely. Sustain is part of a family of MIDI messages called *continuous controllers*. Functionally, the sustain message is like an on/off switch, in that a note is either being held or not. Unlike a sustain pedal on an acoustic piano, which can be used in varying degrees, a synthesizer *hold pedal* generates only "on" and "off" commands. The *sustain* MIDI message simply allows the musician to play more notes without physically holding the original notes.

Pitch Bend

Pitch Bend messages can be sent and received via MIDI. When the pitch bend wheel, or lever, is used on the master synthesizer, the appropriate level of pitch bend is sent in real time to the slave, which then immediately mimics the bend.

Modulation

Although any MIDI message that changes a note over time can be called a *modulator*, the term *modulation* usually refers to an effect similar to vibrato. This information can be sent and received via MIDI. The information sent from the master is received and mimicked by the slave synthesizer.

Volume

Though MIDI messages aren't actual sound, they can control the sound of a MIDI instrument. With the *volume* message, it's possible to control the output volume of a slave MIDI instrument(s) from the master. This can be done using a knob or slider on the front panel of the master/controller, or using a foot pedal connected to the *master*.

Pan

Another useful MIDI continuous controller message is *pan* or *pan pot*. This makes it possible to balance the output of a synthesizer in a stereo sound system. Values of 0–63 will place more sound in the left speaker, while values of 64–127 will place more sound in the right. This is particularly useful in a MIDI *sequencing* application, which will be covered in Chapter Four.

Program Change

This message tells a synthesizer to switch from one patch to another. This makes it possible for a master synthesizer, or sequencer, to control patch selection on any number of slave synthesizers. A program change message points to a specific patch number, but the type of patch residing at that number is determined by the slave synthesizer.

MIDI Connections

MIDI ports

Now that we've defined MIDI and common MIDI messages, it's time to learn how to put this powerful tool to work for us in the real world. It all begins with MIDI Connections or, perhaps better stated, "How do we hook all this stuff up?" Fear not! Setting up a simple MIDI configuration is easier, and perhaps even quicker, than you might have imagined. All that's needed to connect two MIDI synthesizers is a single MIDI cable.

In order to understand how MIDI devices are connected, we need to learn how MIDI devices communicate. Most MIDI devices have three MIDI ports that are used for three distinct purposes. It's important to note that MIDI cables are generic and will work in any of the three ports and on any model or make of synthesizer. Let's take a quick look at each of these MIDI ports:

Let's start with **MIDI OUT**. Think of the MIDI OUT as the mouth of the synthesizer, as all of the MIDI messages originate from this port. Since the master synth is the one sending MIDI messages, it does so from its MIDI OUT port.

Next, let's look at **MIDI IN**. Think of this port as the ears of the synthesizer. Therefore, MIDI messages are received by the slave synthesizer via the MIDI IN port.

So, using only MIDI OUT and MIDI IN, we can create a simple MIDI connection between two synthesizers. The master's MIDI OUT is connected to the slave's MIDI IN. Now, any key played on the master will trigger the same note on the slave without the slave being touched. All of the velocity and note information, plus any continuous controller information, like sustain or modulation, will also be carried through the MIDI cable from master to slave. The slave synthesizer plays exactly the same note with all of the same performance characteristics as the master synthesizer (see diagram on pg. 23). The result is the sound of two patches, one from each synthesizer, being layered together. If an acoustic grand piano patch was selected on the master, and an orchestral string section patch was selected on the slave, we would now hear a combination of acoustic piano and string section when a note is played on the master synthesizer.

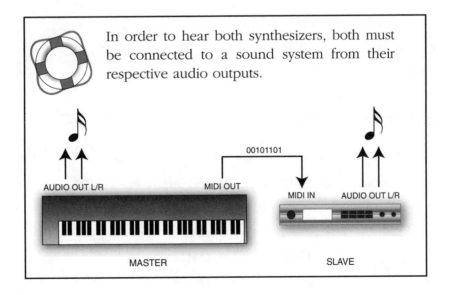

In order to hear both synthesizers, both must be connected to a sound system from their respective audio outputs.

AUDIO OUT L/R   MIDI OUT   00101101   MIDI IN   AUDIO OUT L/R

MASTER   SLAVE

The last of these three ports is called **MIDI THRU**. This port is unique in that it doesn't send its own messages like MIDI OUT, and it doesn't receive MIDI messages like the MIDI IN port. The MIDI THRU port on a synthesizer simply takes what is received from the MIDI IN port and passes it on to another device. This enables more than two MIDI devices to be connected. The master controller sends MIDI messages from its MIDI OUT port to the MIDI IN on a slave synthesizer. That slave synthesizer can then re-send or "echo" that same information (received from the master) to another slave synthesizer. This is accomplished by connecting another MIDI cable from the MIDI THRU port on the first slave synthesizer to the MIDI IN port on the second slave. In this scenario, when a note is played on the master, all three synthesizers will play their respective patches, resulting in an even bigger MIDI layer. This technique can be repeated over and over again, chaining several synthesizers together and creating thick, lush layers of sound. However, be careful in choosing patches to layer. Otherwise, you may find that the cumulative sound of many synthesizers and sound modules can become heavy and muddy sounding.

Connecting Two Synthesizers

A MIDI cable is connected from the MIDI OUT of the master keyboard to the MIDI IN of the slave keyboard. Performance information from the master is automatically sent to the slave, which then mimics the master.

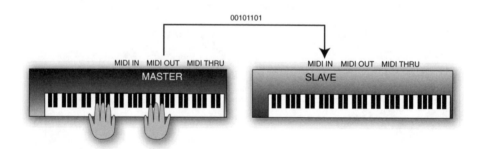

Connecting a Synthesizer to a Sound Module

Sound modules are essentially MIDI keyboards *without the keyboard*. Because the slave doesn't need to be physically played in a MIDI setup, it doesn't necessarily need its own keyboard. Therefore, it is often very cost-effective to supplement a keyboard synthesizer with a sound module. The best part is that the MIDI connections are exactly the same as connecting two MIDI keyboards.

The MIDI OUT of the master keyboard is connected to the MIDI IN of the sound module. This produces the same effect as if two keyboards were connected in this manner. The sound from the master and slave are combined to create a MIDI layer, assuming they're *both* plugged in to the sound system (see illustration on pg. 27).

Connecting Three MIDI Synthesizers

To connect three MIDI synthesizers, you'll need two MIDI cables. The first MIDI connection is identical to what we've done previously. The MIDI OUT of the master is connected to the MIDI IN of the first slave. To connect a third device, the MIDI THRU of the first slave is connected to the MIDI IN port of the second slave—which happens to be a sound module in our diagram. The end result is a MIDI layer of all three synthesizers.

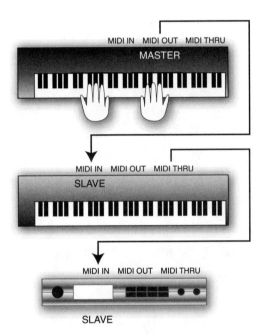

Common Wiring Errors

The most common mistake people make when trying to connect three MIDI devices comes from confusion between the MIDI OUT and MIDI THRU ports. Remember, MIDI OUT is like a *mouth* and is the origin of all the MIDI messages that are sent. MIDI THRU just passes on all messages that it receives through its own *ears*, or MIDI IN port. Think of MIDI THRU as the "church gossip" (every church has one). They don't have any information of their own to communicate but only pass on what they've heard from others. But, while gossip can be a hurtful thing, MIDI THRU is a very helpful thing!

In this illustration, *Keyboard #1* is functioning as the master and is connected correctly to *Keyboard #2,* the first slave synthesizer. But *Keyboard #2* is incorrectly connected to the second slave synthesizer: the *sound module.* The MIDI OUT of *Keyboard #2* is connected to the MIDI IN of the sound module. The end result of the incorrect setup is as follows:

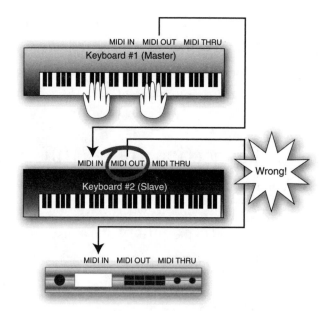

Keyboard #1, when played, would send MIDI messages to *Keyboard #2.* So far, so good. But because the second MIDI cable is connected to the MIDI OUT port on *Keyboard #2,* the MIDI messages sent from *Keyboard #1,* the master, would not be passed on to the sound module. When *Keyboard #1* is played, we would hear *Keyboard #2* as well; but the sound module would be silent. However, in this configuration, if *Keyboard #2* were physically played, it would send its own MIDI messages to the sound module. This would create a MIDI layer between *Keyboard #2* and the sound module. When *Keyboard #2* is physically played, it essentially becomes the master to the module. No messages would be sent to *Keyboard #1,* as there is no connection to its MIDI IN port. If the goal is to layer all three synths, the correct connection would be from the MIDI THRU port on *Keyboard #2* to the MIDI IN of the sound module.

***

So far in this chapter, we've learned what MIDI is, as well as what MIDI *isn't.* We've learned common terms and MIDI messages. We've even learned how to connect MIDI devices. But there is another part of MIDI technology that we've yet to unpack: *MIDI channels.* In the next few pages, we'll gain a basic understanding as to what MIDI channels are. We'll also be unpacking how MIDI channels are used throughout this book. So again, fear not! All will be made clear in good time. Let's begin.

:::::::::MIDI Channels

We know from Chapter Two that *monophonic* synthesizers are only capable of playing a single note at a time, while *polyphonic* synthesizers can play as many notes as their *polyphony* limits will allow. We also learned that a synthesizer's ability to play more than one instrument, or *patch*, at a time is described by the term: *multitimbral*. Most modern synthesizers are multitimbral synthesizers, and a good number are capable of playing as many as sixteen patches at once! This is where MIDI channels enter the picture. MIDI channels enable specific MIDI messages to be sent to specific patches or MIDI devices.

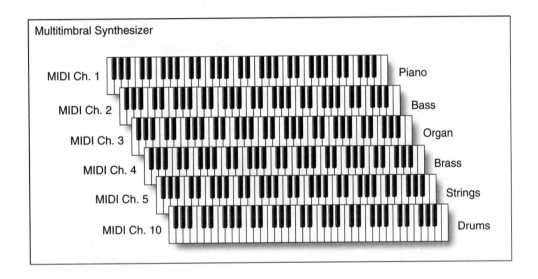

To better understand MIDI channels, think of a television. These days, with cable or satellite-dish technology, many people have access to well over a hundred TV channels. Yet most people view only one program at a time (unless you're like me and watch sports using the picture-in-picture). Your television may be able to access over a hundred programs at once, but each program is broadcast on a different channel to keep things organized. Your television receives these signals, and you choose which one you want to watch by selecting the appropriate channel.

MIDI channels work similarly in that they provide a way to keep MIDI messages organized so that they reach their intended destination. There are a total of sixteen MIDI channels: 1 through 16. You can't watch a television program broadcast on channel two unless your television is tuned to channel two. In the same way, a MIDI message sent on MIDI channel 1 by the *master* will only be properly received if the *slave* device is set to receive on that same channel; in this case, MIDI channel 1. So, the previous illustrations of MIDI connections in this chapter would only be valid if each device was set to send and receive on the same MIDI channel.

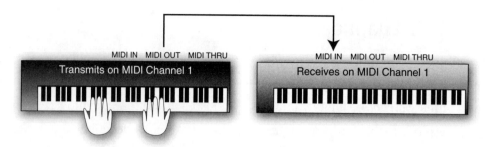

Correct MIDI channel configuration

Most devices can be configured to *send* MIDI messages on one MIDI channel while *receiving* on another. Changing MIDI channels takes only a couple button pushes on most MIDI devices. Many church musicians simply want to layer two or more MIDI devices and have no need for multi-channel MIDI setups. Therefore, they may rarely venture outside MIDI channel 1. Most keyboards are set to send and receive on MIDI channel 1 at the factory. But, as we will discover in the coming chapters, multitimbral synthesizers open up even more musical possibilities for church musicians.

So now that we've learned a little about making MIDI connections, how can we apply it? Here are several real-world ways MIDI technology can enhance your worship ministry:

Layering synthesizers using a MIDI connection conserves polyphony.

We discovered in Chapter Two that each tone inside a patch utilizes a single note of polyphony. Therefore, a six-note chord playing a four-tone patch is actually using 24 notes of polyphony. If we layer another four-tone patch with the first patch via a MIDI connection, we are effectively doubling the texture of the sound, yet we are still only using 24 notes of polyphony per synthesizer. Each synthesizer has its own computer processor, and, therefore, its own polyphony. The master synthesizer is merely controlling the slave synthesizer. So, a slave synthesizer generates its own sounds and polyphony as well.

MIDI keeps your controller from becoming obsolete. One of the greatest concerns people have when purchasing electronics these days is that the technology could be obsolete by the time it's taken out of the box. While that's a bit of an overstatement, the fact is, acoustic instruments have traditionally enjoyed a longer life span than their electronic counterparts. But today's MIDI instruments are closing the gap quickly.

Picture the following scenario: An 88-key synthesizer with piano-like weighted action was purchased five years ago. Today, it still has a nice feel, but the patches are starting to sound dated. Current technology allows for more faithful reproductions of acoustic instruments as well as new sound capabilities that were not found on synthesizers five years ago. One might think that it's time to replace the 88-key synthesizer with a newer version at considerable expense. While that's certainly an option, there is a less expensive option that will yield equal if not superior results!

In Chapter Two, we learned about sound modules. These are essentially synthesizers without the keyboard. These box-shaped instruments often have sound libraries that are identical to or bigger than a keyboard synthesizer made by the same manufacturer. Because the manufacturer is able to construct a smaller product without the expense of adding a mechanized keyboard and other performance-related controls, the price of a sound module is usually considerably lower than its keyboard counterpart. But here's the great part: By creating a MIDI connection between the five-year old, 88-key synthesizer (as master) and the new sound module (as slave), we now have access to all of the new and improved sounds in the sound module.

Roland's Fantom-XR module has more sounds and is more expandable than the 88-key Roland XV-88 keyboard synthesizer. And yet the Fantom-XR is smaller, easier to transport, and costs less than half of the retail price of a new 88-note synthesizer.

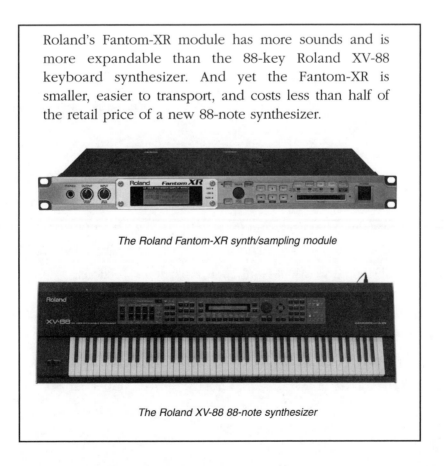

The Roland Fantom-XR synth/sampling module

The Roland XV-88 88-note synthesizer

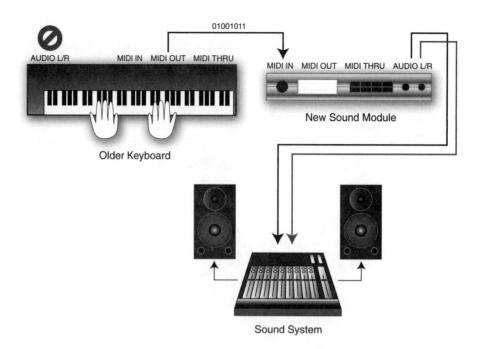

01001011

AUDIO L/R   MIDI IN   MIDI OUT   MIDI THRU   MIDI IN   MIDI OUT   MIDI THRU   AUDIO L/R

New Sound Module

Older Keyboard

Sound System

Here's how the connections would look. Since the 88-key synthesizer has keys, it has to be the master. Since the sound module has no keys, and no way to be physically played, it cannot be the master. Therefore, the sound module must be the slave. In order to send MIDI messages from the master, we'll need to use the MIDI *mouth* of the keyboard, connecting a MIDI cable to its MIDI OUT port. In order for the slave to receive or *hear* the MIDI messages, we'll need to use the MIDI *ear* of the sound module, so we'll connect the other end of the MIDI cable to the module's MIDI IN port. If both the keyboard and sound module are connected to the sound system, then we have just created a MIDI layer. In other words, both devices will play when a key is pressed. However, in this situation, we don't want to create a MIDI layer. Because the master keyboard in our example is dated and may not have the kinds of sounds that we're looking for, we may choose not to connect it to the sound system at all. In the example above, the MIDI OUT of the master keyboard is connected to the MIDI IN of the sound module, but only the sound module is connected to the sound system. Though both devices are actually playing notes, only the sound module will be heard. Remember, *MIDI is not sound.* No sound is transmitted via MIDI—only performance instructions.

Sound modules are often considerably less expensive than their keyboard-based counterparts. And, while purchasing a new keyboard can run as high as $2,000 or more, adding a sound module to an existing MIDI keyboard (as in the above example) can provide a state-of-the-art sound library for well under $1,000.

The Crossing, a large contemporary church in Costa Mesa, California, has found a way to stay current as well as stretch their financial investment. Instead of replacing keyboards when they begin to grow obsolete, they've elected to purchase less-expensive sound modules as MIDI "add-ons" to their existing equipment. Rather than spending $3,500 on a single replacement keyboard, the director of music was able to purchase three sound modules for about the same amount! Having more than one sound module also allows him to utilize more than one keyboard player in a service. Keyboard players on the worship team at The Crossing can be seen playing a Roland D-20 or a JV-80—both keyboards over ten years old. These seemingly obsolete keyboards are given new life when connected via MIDI to a Roland JV-1080, a Roland JV-2080, or a Roland JV-1010 sound module. The D-20 and JV-80 keyboards are not even connected to the sound system. Instead they're acting solely as controllers, sending note and performance information to the sound modules, which, of course, are connected to the sound system.

Here's another way to create a win-win situation using your older keyboard—a win for your music, and a win for your ministry. Let's say there's another keyboardist you've been wanting to give an opportunity to serve, but they're just not ready to be the sole keyboardist. Or, you've got a stable of players, and you'd love to be able to utilize more than one-at-a-time. You can update your older keyboard and get another player involved in one step. In the same way that a sound module can revitalize an older MIDI keyboard, a new keyboard can do that too, and at the same time provide another instrument to play. Assuming the new keyboard is multitimbral, it can receive MIDI messages from the older keyboard to trigger one sound, and from its own keyboard, trigger a different one.

So, in the first scenario, the seasoned keyboardist could play the older keyboard (*master*)—triggering a piano patch residing in the new keyboard (*slave*). Meanwhile, the new keyboardist plays the new keyboard—playing simple whole notes on a lush string pad. In the scenario where you have two accomplished players, the options are wide open. The older keyboard can trigger a split of organ and electric piano in the new keyboard via MIDI, while the other player plays brass and strings from the new keyboard itself. Chances are, the new keyboard has multiple audio outputs, so you could still mix each player individually in the sound system.

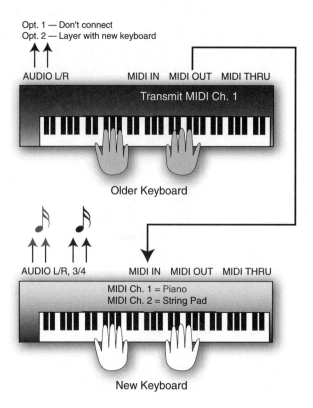

This same concept can also be applied with any steel-string guitar or bass using a Roland GK-series pickup.

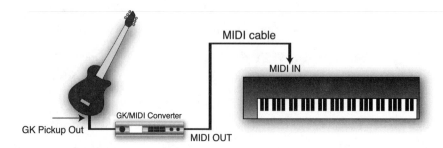

Now it's time to take a deep breath and, if you can reach, pat yourself on the back. We've just completed most of the really technical stuff. We've learned about synthesizers and begun developing the vocabulary that goes with the territory. We've learned what MIDI is, what it's not, and, perhaps more importantly, how to hook it up! We've even touched on a few practical tips along the way. Now it's time to shift our focus a bit as we explore some very practical applications of electronic music technology in worship. In the next chapter, we'll learn how to create recorded MIDI keyboard tracks for worship or rehearsal. We'll also learn how to record and print music using a personal computer. And, of course, we'll learn how to hook it up!

FOUR

MIDI SEQUENCING IN A WORSHIP CONTEXT

Learning about music technology can be compared to climbing a mountain. The process of climbing, though challenging, has its rewards along the way. But when the summit is finally reached, the view from the top makes it all worthwhile. During our climb, we've been ascending through new concepts and a new vocabulary. But now that we've tackled the synthesizer and the basics of how MIDI works, we're ready to reach the summit and take a look around.

The first three chapters can be summarized as "what" chapters, answering questions like, "What is electronic music?" "What is a synthesizer?" and "What is MIDI?" Beginning with this chapter, we'll shift away from the "what" and instead focus on the "how to." The rest of this book is primarily focused on providing practical tips on how specific areas of music technology can enhance the worship life of your congregation.

Our shift toward the "how to" begins with *MIDI Sequencing*. A *MIDI Sequencer*, which is usually just called a "sequencer," records and plays back MIDI information much like a tape recorder plays back sound. But, while a tape recorder records actual sound, a sequencer records and plays back MIDI information; in fact, the same MIDI messages we learned about in Chapter Three. When a sequencer is connected to a synthesizer, you can record and play music much like a tape recorder but with much more flexibility.

It might help to think of a sequencer like a word processor for MIDI messages. In the same way that word processors offer tremendous flexibility and infinite editing capability for writers, sequencers offer these benefits to musicians.

Because a sequencer is dealing with digital MIDI messages only (as opposed to analog sound), a musician has a great deal of control over the music being sequenced. For example, unlike a tape recorder, a sequencer can change the tempo without changing the pitch of a song. A sequencer can also change the pitch without changing the tempo. Individual MIDI messages can be examined and even changed, making it possible to change notes, correct rhythms, and fix mistakes with the click of a mouse or the push of a couple of buttons. A sequencer can even mimic a multi-track recorder by sequencing different instruments on different MIDI channels. This allows a sequencer and a multitimbral synthesizer to create full orchestrations that rival the size and depth of a symphony orchestra!

Your head may be spinning with possibilities right now. That's a good thing! MIDI sequencing can be an amazing tool to enhance worship music. In the next few pages, we'll learn about:

- Recording, playback, and editing
- Types of sequencers
- Standard MIDI Files
- Sequencing in a worship context
- Music notation software

Also, keep your eye out for a Ministry Snapshot to see how church musicians around the country are utilizing sequencers in powerful ways.

Although sequencers come in various packages, they operate pretty much the same way. Some sequencers, like the Roland MC-80 (pictured below) are stand-alone devices. Other sequencers are built into keyboards called "workstations," like the Roland Fantom-X8 (pictured above). Logic, from Emagic, is an example of a software-based sequencer.

Recording, Playing, and Editing

Let's go back to the analogy we made about sequencers and word processors. Instead of having to create a perfect document by hand, a word processor allows us to experiment. We can change letters, words, and paragraphs quickly to suit our needs. We can change the font without changing anything else. There is little doubt that the power and speed of the word processor has greatly enhanced our ability to write.

A sequencer is like a word processor, in that changes can be made quickly and easily *after* the music has already been recorded. In fact, sequencing has borrowed the ability to copy, cut, and paste from the world of computers. If we need to repeat a musical phrase several times, there's no need to play it over and over. We can play it once, *copy* it, and *paste* it to create the correct number of measures. If we play a wrong note, there's no need to start over. A sequencer allows us the ability to change or even delete a single note without affecting the notes around it.

But let's not get ahead of ourselves. Let's look at how sequencers record and play music. For this example, let's assume that the sequencer is built into a multitimbral keyboard. This keyboard would be called a "workstation" because it has a built-in sequencer. Since this keyboard is a "workstation," there is no need for any other MIDI equipment or cables. Of course, the keyboard would need to be connected to an amplifier, P.A. system, or headphones in order to be heard. We'll take a more in-depth look at workstations later in this chapter.

At the heart of any sequencer is a *clock*, which is used to control the timing and tempo of the sequence. The clock will create a *click track*, which is essentially a *metronome* that shows us where the beat is. The clock can be set to virtually any tempo. And because the tempo can be changed later with no ill effects, it can be set to suit the keyboard player's comfort zone—even if it's well below performance tempo! Most sequencers can be set to include *count-off measures* of various lengths. Many sequencers can also be configured to begin recording automatically when it senses that you've begun playing. The important thing to remember here, is that sequencers are highly flexible and can be configured to reflect your own personal work style as it develops.

So let's assume that we've set up our sequencer to have a one-measure count-off and a tempo of 60 beats per minute (BPM). This slow tempo will help us play a difficult passage successfully. Because sequencers have *transport* buttons similar to a tape recorder (play, stop, record, etc.), it's easy to record. So, we press the record button and immediately hear the metronome click, which is set at 60 BPM. After the one-measure count off, we begin playing. Let's assume, in our example, that we play everything correctly except for a single note in our left hand. Instead of playing an F-natural, *we played an F-sharp!* As a result, we became a bit frustrated and our timing was a little off after the mistake. Well, here's the best part about sequencing: *We don't have to record the song again!* We can simply fix our mistakes by editing our sequence. In fact, once you get the hang of it, editing a song like this can be done in less than a minute!

Virtually all sequencers have an editing menu that allows us to view all of the MIDI information, which includes the specific notes that we played. If we know that we played a wrong note at measure eight, all we need to do is view that measure in the editing menu. A quick glance is all that is necessary to locate the erroneous F-sharp that we played. If the F-sharp is unwanted altogether, we can simply *select* it, then press *delete*, and the note will be erased. However, in our case, we mistakenly played the F-sharp instead of an F-natural. So, we select the F-sharp and change it to an F-natural. Once we get familiar with our sequencer's menu layout, we can, most likely, accomplish a simple edit like this in less than 15 seconds. If we had to play the song again to fix the mistake, it would likely take much longer. Most music ministers I know would love to have a few extra minutes each day. Sequencing just might help make that happen!

Quantizing

But, wait, our example is not finished yet. You'll recall that we had some timing problems after the mistake we made at measure eight. Today's sequencers are so powerful, that we could edit the timing of each note individually. But that might take awhile—especially if our song has a lot of eighth or sixteenth notes. There's a better way to accomplish this task. It's called *quantizing*.

Because a sequencer uses a clock to control timing and tempo, it takes a very accurate picture of the notes that we play and *when* we play them. In other words, not only can a sequencer differentiate between note names and duration, a sequencer can also keep tabs on how accurately we played each note in relationship to the tempo (click track). In the same way that a metronome divides a minute into beats per minute (BPM), a sequencer divides a beat into a specific number of *clock ticks*. This number is usually referred to as the sequencer's *resolution*, or *PPQN (Parts Per Quarter Note)*. Most of today's sequencers have a resolution of at least 480 PPQN. At this resolution a quarter note represents 480 clock ticks, a half note is 960 clock ticks, an eighth note is 240 clock ticks, and a sixteenth note is 120 clock ticks.

Why do we need so many clock ticks? Because the higher the sequencer's resolution, the less "machine-like" the music will sound. The truth is, great music is *not* perfect music. If we played every note exactly right on the beat, music would sound mechanical and uninteresting. Therefore, today's sequencers give us enough resolution to play as sloppily, and musically, as we wish! Now, back to our timing problem.

So what is *quantization?* Simply put, quantization is a sequencer's ability to automatically correct the timing of the notes we play. If, in our example, we meant to play two consecutive eighth notes beginning on beat one, our editing menu would show two notes. The first note would read: *beat 1, clock tick 0*. The second note would read: *beat 1, clock tick 240*, that is, if we played perfectly. Chances are we didn't play perfectly. Rather, we were a bit behind the beat. Our editing menu might read something like: *beat 1, clock tick 40* and *beat 1, clock tick 290*. This is where quantizing comes in. Quantization allows us to correct the timing in a section of music, or even an entire song, in a single button push or click of the mouse. We simply tell the sequencer that we meant to play eighth notes, and the sequencer will quantize the notes to the correct values.

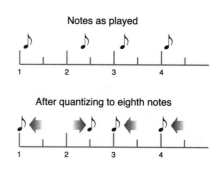

One of the best features in modern sequencers is the ability to *scale* the influence of quantization. Remember, perfect music is probably mechanical-sounding music. So we may not want to change the note values to a perfect position. Rather, we might want the notes to be *off* a bit, but not too much—only enough to give the music a nice *feel*. Most sequencers allow us to adjust the *strength* of the quantization—the degree to which quantization changes a note's timing. In our example, our first eighth note landed at *clock 40* and our second eighth note landed at *clock 290* of beat one—this is well behind the beat. So we'll want the sequencer to play back each note earlier. If we instruct the sequencer to quantize at 100 percent, the notes will snap back to the *perfect* values of *clock 0* and *clock 240*, which is probably undesirable. However, if we instruct the sequencer to quantize at 50 percent *strength*, each note will move half way toward its mathematically perfect destination. Because our first eighth note is late by 40 clocks, quantizing at 50 percent would move it to *clock 20*. Our second eighth note is late by 50 clocks, so quantizing at 50 percent would move it to *clock 265*.

If all this math is intimidating, don't worry. In reality, quantizing a sequence is very easy to do and takes only a couple button pushes or clicks of the mouse. You don't need to be a math whiz to figure out what the right setting will be—use your ear for that. Most sequencers give you the ability to audition quantization settings without permanently changing the timing. Therefore, the best bet is to just fiddle around a bit until you get something that sounds good to you. After quantizing a few tracks, you'll begin to figure out what settings work best for your playing.

 When trying to sequence a difficult song, slow the tempo down to a manageable pace. This will enable you to play the song with more accuracy and musicality than if you had tried to sequence it at full speed. Once you've finished recording your part and doing any necessary editing, bring the tempo back to the original setting. You'll sound like a pro, and nobody will know your secret!

Tempo and Key Changes

As we learned earlier in this chapter, it is possible to change keys (pitch) and tempo independently in a MIDI sequence. The important thing to remember here is that a sequencer is only recording MIDI messages, not actual *sound*. Therefore, transposing the key or changing the tempo is as simple as changing the font size in a word processor.

Controllers

In Chapter Three, we learned about modulation and pitch bend. These are examples of MIDI messages called MIDI Controllers. They are performance messages that change a sound over time. MIDI Volume is another controller. Sustain, or hold, is another controller. If a controller is used in a performance, the MIDI data generated by the controller will be recorded in real time by a MIDI sequencer. This is not something that you need to learn how to do. Your sequencer does it automatically for you! Once recorded, controller information can be edited in the same way that note information is edited. For example, if you're a little sloppy with the sustain pedal, just go in and change the timing of the sustain *on* and *off* messages. It's really that simple.

MIDI sequencing can be used to create instrument parts when there are no musicians available. Like most churches, Glen Ellyn Bible Church in Glen Ellyn, Illinois, doesn't have an overabundance of musicians. But that doesn't keep their worship band from sounding like a large ensemble. Jason Sirvatka, director of worship ministries, regularly creates sequences to supplement the church's worship band when musicians aren't available. If he needs a violin player, or even an entire string section, he just creates a sequence for the band to play along with. In order to ensure that the worship band stays in time with the sequence tempo, the drummer listens to a click track through headphones in the service.

Jason also uses sequencing when rehearsing his vocal team. Rather than fumbling around on the keyboard, trying to find the best key for a soloist, Jason creates a simple sequence that can be easily transposed at the click of the mouse in order to find the right key. Jason is then freed up from playing "accompanist" and is able to focus on leading the vocal rehearsal.

:::::::Tracks and MIDI Channels

We've already learned that multitimbral synthesizers are capable of playing more than one patch at a time. This capability benefits MIDI sequencing greatly! When using a multitimbral synthesizer, you can to create MIDI compositions (sequences) that use several patches simultaneously. However, instead of layering the patches, you can have each patch play its own designated part. For example, after you record a piano part, you may want to add a string section to add depth to the music. However, you probably don't want the strings to copy the piano part note-for-note. Sequencing with a multitimbral synthesizer gives you the ability to record a completely different string part while listening to the original piano part. However, the sequencer is only able to distinguish between the parts *if* they're played on different MIDI channels. This is accomplished on the sequencer *and* on the synthesizer. Each has to be configured properly. For example, Track 1 on a sequencer is usually set up to automatically record MIDI channel 1. So if you want your piano part to go on Track 1, the synthesizer has to be set up with a piano patch that is receiving on MIDI channel 1.

If you want to add strings, you'll need to tell the sequencer to record on Track 2—which can be set up to record any MIDI channel—but we'll choose MIDI channel 2 just to keep it simple. The synthesizer would then need to be configured so that there is a string patch, which receives on MIDI channel 2. This can be repeated again and again, using all sixteen MIDI channels. In fact, the only real limitation is polyphony. But then again, as we've already learned, we can always add another MIDI instrument—such as a sound module—to gain more polyphony and, for that matter, more MIDI channels.

Track Number	Instrument Name	MIDI Ch.	
Track 1	Piano	1	
Track 2	Bass	2	
Track 3	Organ	3	
Track 4	Strings	4	
Track 5	Horns	5	
Track 6	Synth 1	6	
Track 7	Synth 2	7	
Track 8	Drums	10	

A basic sequencer track display

These examples have been based on using a sequencer that is built into a multi-timbral keyboard synthesizer (workstation). Though a workstation often does a lot of the configuration for you automatically, the same concepts apply to any sequencer. Sequencers can take on several different shapes and sizes. Let's take a look at the various types of sequencers, along with the unique benefits of each type.

Keyboard Workstations

Any MIDI keyboard that has a sequencer onboard is called a *workstation*. Because sequencers record and play back MIDI data, building a sequencer into a MIDI keyboard is a natural fit. The name "workstation" comes from the fact that everything we might need to create a sequence is completely integrated into one device. There is no need for extra MIDI cables, a computer, software, or a MIDI interface. There is very little configuration, if any, needed. It's a turnkey approach to MIDI and, as a result, a very popular option for those looking to create music using a sequencer.

The Roland Fantom-X8 workstation contains great sounds, a large color display, powerful sequencing capabilities, and the ability to store sequences internally or to your computer via a USB connection.

While early workstations were somewhat difficult to use due to small displays and clumsy interfaces, today's workstations are extremely powerful instruments. Many current workstations have large back-lit displays that provide graphic, friendly controls for recording and editing. Virtually all workstations have the ability to store sequences to some sort of a storage medium—like a media card or floppy disk.

What are a workstation's advantages over other types of sequencers? One of the main advantages is complete integration of the sequencer and the synthesizer. There will never be any incompatibility between the hardware and the software. There are no software authorizations or keys to keep track of, or drivers to update. Workstations power on and are ready to go very quickly with one power switch and only one power cable. Another advantage is that a workstation is portable. Using a MIDI sequence in a live-performance situation is easily accomplished using a workstation. The key word here is "convenience."

What are the disadvantages of workstations? The truth is that with every passing year, the disadvantages get smaller and smaller. It used to be that workstations were not as powerful as their computer software–based counterparts. And while computers still hold an advantage over workstations in terms of sheer processing power and display size, the fact is that there are very few things a musician cannot do with a good workstation.

Software-based Sequencers

The rise of the personal computer has brought unprecedented capabilities to the average person. The world of electronic music is no exception. Software used for sequencing has been around since the mid-1980s. Like workstations, the early software was awkward and not very intuitive. However, today's music software offers powerful, user-friendly tools that are within just about any church's music budget.

Digital Performer, by MOTU, is a powerful sequencing tool, yet has an intuitive, user-friendly graphic interface.

Unlike workstations, where everything needed is integrated into a single device, sequencing software is dependent on a few other factors: a computer, a MIDI interface, MIDI cables (at least two), and a MIDI synthesizer. Let's look at each of the components in a computer-based MIDI setup.

The Computer

While a well-programmed MIDI sequence is a very powerful thing indeed, sequencing software is not particularly draining on a computer's processor or RAM (short-term memory). That's good news for many of us who are using older computers. But, as with just about anything else, a faster computer with more RAM will probably result in a more fulfilling experience. Many sequencing software applications also have the ability to create a printable music score (more on that later in this chapter). Some sequencing software integrates the ability to record and play back sound (audio) along with MIDI sequences. This allows you to add recordings of vocals or other acoustic instrument to MIDI sequences. This is called *hard disk recording* because actual sound is digitized and recorded to the computer's hard disk (long-term memory). We've dedicated an entire chapter to hard disk recording in this book. For now, it's important to note that hard disk recording requires a very fast computer with a great deal of RAM and hard disk space. So if you're planning on using sequencing software that integrates hard disk recording into its capabilities, you'll want to make sure your computer is up to the task.

When I teach workshops on this subject, inevitably the topic of whether sequencing is better performed on a Windows-based PC or on an Apple Macintosh comes up. It is true that in the early days of music software, the Mac was the clear choice of music professionals. However, in recent years the playing field has leveled dramatically. As a somewhat typical Mac user, I'm very passionate about my computer and believe that everyone should own a Mac. However, the truth is that *each person would be better served by using the platform with which he or she is most comfortable.* So to end the controversy here and now, let's be completely clear on this: It really doesn't matter which platform you use! And as we'll learn a bit later in this chapter, MIDI sequence files can easily be shared between platforms, thus making the specific platform less important in the long run.

MIDI Cables/MIDI Interface

Computers make great musical tools. However, there's one problem: Computers don't speak MIDI without some help. If you examine your computer closely, you'll notice that your computer does not have a MIDI port built in. And, while computers are becoming more and more intuitive, they haven't quite reached the point where they can read our minds. So we'll have to help them out a bit by attaching a MIDI interface. Simply put, a MIDI interface is a device that allows a computer to communicate with MIDI devices. MIDI interfaces typically have at least one MIDI IN port and one MIDI OUT port. However, it's not uncommon for MIDI interfaces to have multiple IN and OUT ports. Since each MIDI port can support a maximum of 16 MIDI channels, more ports can mean more MIDI channels. More MIDI channels means more patches on more synthesizers that can play more individual parts for bigger, more robust orchestrations.

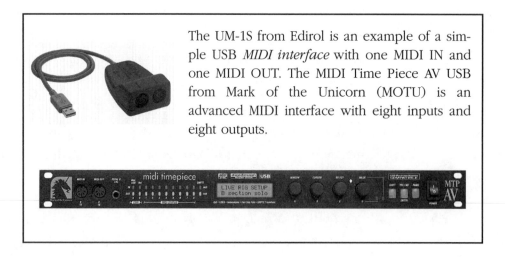

The UM-1S from Edirol is an example of a simple USB *MIDI interface* with one MIDI IN and one MIDI OUT. The MIDI Time Piece AV USB from Mark of the Unicorn (MOTU) is an advanced MIDI interface with eight inputs and eight outputs.

MIDI interfaces come in several shapes and sizes. The main differences being:

- How many IN and OUT ports does it have?
- How does it connect to the computer?

For most of us, an interface with a single IN port and two or three OUT ports will suffice. How your interface connects to your computer has more to do with what computer you have. Some PC computers come with sound cards that have a 13-pin *game port*. A generic cable from your local computer store can convert the game port into MIDI IN and MIDI OUT cables. However, most current MIDI interfaces rely on a USB connection. USB, or Universal Serial Bus, has become the standard on today's computers, and whether you know it or not, you're probably already using USB to connect your printer, scanner, or even your PDA to the computer.

As far as MIDI cables go, you'll need at least two. You may need more, depending on the number of synthesizers in your setup. MIDI cables come in varying lengths, but the shorter the better. As the diagram below shows, one MIDI cable connects the MIDI OUT on the synthesizer to the MIDI IN on the MIDI interface. This connection allows the synthesizer to send MIDI information to the sequencing software for recording. However, if we stop there, the computer will not be able to send information back to the synthesizer to trigger its sounds. Therefore we must connect the MIDI OUT on the MIDI interface to the MIDI IN on the synthesizer. In our diagram, the MIDI interface is connected to the computer via its USB port. A standard USB cable is usually included with the MIDI interface or permanently attached to it. A single USB cable carries MIDI messages in both directions from the computer to the interface and back.

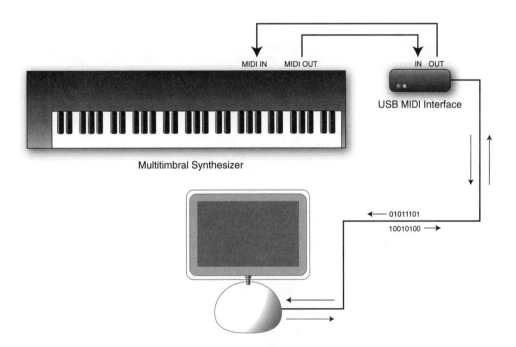

If you're going to sequence with software on a computer, there's an important feature on your keyboard that you need to understand called *local control*. When your keyboard is attached to your computer via MIDI and you're running sequencing software, the synthesizer inside your keyboard will receive messages from two sources: MIDI IN and *locally* (the actual keys on your keyboard). This being the case, when you play the keyboard you'll hear a strange "phasing" or "flanging" sound because the synth is trying to play two of the same note at almost the exact same time. Or, when you're trying to play a string patch, you also hear drums or something else on top of it. It's like the effect created when someone calls into a radio station and they have their radio turned on at home. The DJ always says, "Turn your radio off." So that's what we have to do—turn local control off. With local control off, the keyboard will be effectively disconnected from its internal synthesizer, leaving only MIDI messages sent from MIDI OUT, routed through the software and back to MIDI IN to trigger sounds. If all of this sounds too confusing, don't worry, just turn local control off when you're sequencing with software, and turn it back on when you're not.

What are the advantages of using sequencing software? One advantage is that, unlike many workstations, sequencing software is continually updated over time. Chances are very good that you'll be able to grow with the technology by upgrading your software over time. Another advantage is that, because computers generally outpace synthesizers in terms of raw processing power, choosing a software-based sequencer may keep you ahead of the technology curve. However, while the gap between computers and workstations used to be quite wide, the distance is decreasing rapidly. One of the most popular advantages to using a software sequencer is that the display is limited only by your budget. While workstations now have bigger displays than ever, even the top-of-the-line workstations pale in comparison to some of the large LCD monitors available for computers. It's not even uncommon to have a computer with two display monitors. This allows you to customize your desktop, ensuring that important windows and menus are constantly viewable. Additionally, sequencing software is a good choice for those who want to integrate hard disk recording with MIDI and/or create printable music scores.

What are the disadvantages of sequencing software? The main disadvantages are found in the lack of integration that workstations enjoy. As a result, a considerable investment is required—especially for those starting from scratch. Another disadvantage of software-based sequencers is the lack of portability. Unless you have a laptop computer, it's quite a hassle to move a computer system around regularly. Even with a laptop, there's still other hardware to deal with including a MIDI interface, MIDI cables, power supplies, etc. For most worship applications, laptops simply don't offer the convenience afforded by a keyboard workstation.

Stand-alone Hardware Sequencers

While most of today's sequencers are either workstations or software-based sequencers, many of the early sequencers were stand-alone hardware sequencers. These tabletop devices connect to keyboard synthesizers via MIDI cables. A stand-alone hardware sequencer is basically a workstation with no keyboard and no sounds. Most hardware sequencers work identically to those found in workstations but they can be used with any MIDI keyboard synthesizer. The figure below shows such a connection:

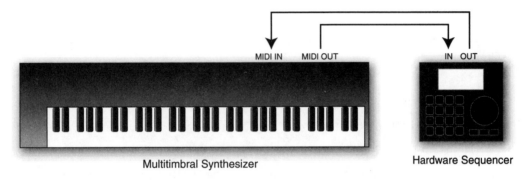

Multitimbral Synthesizer   Hardware Sequencer

Advantages to hardware sequencers are mainly found in portability. Although there are relatively few hardware sequencers available today, many musicians continue to find them to be a powerful part of their MIDI setups.

The Roland MC-80 is an example of a stand-alone hardware sequencer. This sequencer has many of the same powerful editing capabilities that are found in professional software-based sequencers. Other benefits include the option of installing a hard drive to store hundreds of sequences for quick retrieval. The MC-80 can also be upgraded with a sound expansion board so it can act as a sequencer and sound module.

Standard MIDI Files

In Chapter Three, we learned how MIDI arose from a need to create a standard that allowed devices to communicate with each other, regardless of the manufacturer. Shortly after the introduction of MIDI, the need arose for a *file format* that allowed sequences created on one device or software program, to play back on a different device or program. The Standard MIDI File (SMF) was the answer designed to meet that need. Today, most sequencers provide two options when saving a file. The first option is to save it as a proprietary file that can only be opened in that particular sequencer. The second option is to save the file as a Standard MIDI File. All MIDI messages are kept intact in a Standard MIDI File. These include note information, patch information, tempo information, and controllers. When saving a Standard MIDI File, the file name must always end with the ".MID" extension. This identifies the file as a Standard MIDI File to any software- or hardware-based sequencer that tries to read it.

There are two types of Standard MIDI File: Type 0 and Type 1. Type 0 stores all 16 channels of MIDI information on a single track. Type 1 keeps each MIDI channel separate on individual tracks. Both file types also have a separate tempo track. When you choose to save a sequence as a Standard MIDI File, you may be asked to select which type you prefer. If you're going to be attaching the file in an email or uploading it to the Internet, save it as a Type 0 file. If not, save it as Type 1.

While Standard MIDI Files are compatible with virtually any sequencer, they don't always play back with the correct sounds. For example, let's assume that we've created a sequence on a workstation and then saved it to a floppy disk as a Standard MIDI File. We'd like to play that SMF on another workstation made by a different manufacturer. While the Standard MIDI File is compatible with both devices, there are still some potential challenges.

The problem is that the sound libraries of different synthesizers are not identical. In our example, let's assume that we created our sequence using preset piano patch #1 and recorded it on MIDI channel 1. However, on the other workstation, patch #1 is not a piano. In fact, it's some sort of *spacey synth sound*! This is certainly not the effect we were hoping for. Because sequences are essentially a set of MIDI instructions, the actual sounds that are triggered are dependent on the synthesizer that the sequence is being played on. In our example, we could easily change the sound from the *spacey synth sound* to a *piano sound*. But if we had to do that each time we wanted to play a SMF, it would be quite a hassle. Sounds like we need another new standard.

General MIDI

The answer to our compatibility problem is quite simple: Create a standard that each manufacturer must follow that outlines the types of sounds in each synthesizer as well as where each sound lies within its memory banks. This new standard would mandate that patch #1 would always be an *acoustic grand piano* and that patch #110 would always be a *bagpipe*.

It took a lot of negotiating between manufacturers, but ultimately they agreed on a standard called *General MIDI (GM)*. This new standard was an option that manufacturers could add to their synthesizers—essentially an extra bank of standardized sounds. General MIDI includes a list of specifications that all GM capable synthesizers have in common. The list includes:

- *128 preset sounds.* These sounds are always the same in every synthesizer's General MIDI bank. For example, patch #1 is always an acoustic grand piano. Patch #110 is always a bagpipe. While the specific patch locations are the same on any GM compatible device, the quality of each sound is dependent on the particular manufacturer. Not all acoustic grand piano patches are created equally.

- *Multitimbral.* Patches can be played on all 16 MIDI channels simultaneously.

- *24 notes of polyphony*—minimum.

- *Responsive to controllers* such as modulation, volume, sustain pedal, etc.

The introduction of General MIDI has enabled the creation of commercially available MIDI files. Because we can now count on compatibility between sequencers (via Standard MIDI Files) and synthesizers (via General MIDI), we now have the ability to create sequences that just about anyone can play. Many computer games, websites, and software applications also use General MIDI sounds to create music.

Today, companies offer General MIDI-compatible sequences for worship. Praise choruses, hymns, seasonal songs, and even children's music are available to churches that wish to purchase them. These commercial files are sequenced in such a way that no configuration is necessary as long as the playback device is GM compatible.

How do I know if my synthesizer or sound module is General MIDI capable? This very common question is easily answered. General MIDI devices bear the General MIDI logo. It may be small, but if the device is a GM device, the logo will be there somewhere.

It's also important to note that there are several newer standards available. These standards have names like GS or XG. They're not replacements for the GM standards; rather, they are further enhancements of the GM standard. However, these standards are less common and are often restricted to particular manufacturers. But don't worry; if your MIDI file is GM and GS compatible, but your sound module is only GM compatible, the sound module will simply ignore the GS instructions that are embedded in the MIDI file. Of course, then you'll be missing the enhancements afforded by a GS-compatible device.

Recently, a new standard, General MIDI 2, was introduced. This new standard is a further improvement on General MIDI and is being implemented in an ever-increasing number of MIDI devices. General MIDI 2 improves on its predecessor by doubling the number of instruments to 256 and increasing polyphony from 24 notes to 32 notes. At the time of this writing, there are very few, if any, commercially available MIDI files for worship that are optimized for General MIDI 2. However, General MIDI 1 files will play properly on a General MIDI 2 synth. It's best to check your owner's manual or contact the manufacturer should any compatibility issues arise.

Sequencing in a Worship Context

If you're new to MIDI sequencing, then you're probably riding the fence between being "wowed" by the amazing potential of this technology and pondering the fact that it's going to take a little time before you get up to speed. While it is true that sequencing takes a bit of effort to master, the payoff is huge. Let's take a look at some ways that sequencing can enhance worship ministries.

Sequencing to supplement a live ensemble

In churches that already have a healthy supply of gifted musicians, sequencing can be used to add texture or depth to an ensemble. It's important to note that sequencing can be effective in any music style or instrumentation. MIDI sequences can add to an organ-led service as well as to a modern rhythm section that plays contemporary styles of worship.

In order to ensure success when adding a sequence to an existing ensemble, you'll need to provide a tempo reference for the musicians. Otherwise the musicians won't be able to follow the sequence. If your sequence consists of a string section playing a bunch of whole notes, how will the musicians know where the tempo is? This is where a click track comes in handy. In the same way that we play along with a metronome when creating a sequence, we'll need a *click track* to make sure everyone plays in sync. In a contemporary ensemble, this is often accomplished by feeding the click track to the drummer or conductor through headphones. Headphones are chosen so the congregation does not hear the click coming from the stage monitors. Some hardware sequencers and workstations have an audio output dedicated for a click track. This makes setting up a click track very simple. Other sequencers may require you to create your own click track.

How do I create a click track? To create your own click track, add another track to your sequence and choose a percussive patch like castanets or a wood block. The General MIDI standard for percussion is MIDI Channel 10. Most MIDI devices have percussion patches that are pre-configured to send and receive MIDI messages on MIDI channel 10.

Add a track that contains quarter notes on each downbeat. Then quantize these notes at 100 percent strength.

If your synthesizer has multiple audio outputs, configure it to play the click track patch from a different audio output than the rest of the sequence. This allows you to isolate the click track and keep it from being audible to the rest of the congregation.

Another way to accomplish this is to use a separate synth or drum machine for the click. To do this, connect an additional MIDI cable from either the MIDI THRU port on your primary synth or a MIDI OUT port on your MIDI interface (it doesn't matter which one you choose). Set the second synthesizer or drum machine to receive information only on MIDI channel 10. This also isolates the click from the rest of the sequence, as you're essentially delegating one synthesizer for the click track and the other synth for the sequence itself. The next step would typically be to route a set of headphones to the drummer from the *click* synth.

It's amazing to hear what a MIDI sequence can add to even a single musician! It's important to note that it is possible to create a sequence that doesn't need a click track. This is especially helpful when it's not practical to wear headphones to reference a click—as in the case of a solo vocal guitar-playing worship leader. To create a "clickless" sequence, you'll need to create an arrangement that includes some sense of time. This can be accomplished by sequencing an arpeggiated piano part or, perhaps, a simple percussion track. Or, if the style is appropriate, it might involve a full drum kit. The key is to avoid creating measures in your sequence that have no sense of time (such as whole notes). You'll also want to create a lead-in measure so you know where to begin playing. Or, if you're rhythmically savvy, you might be able to get away with a few pickup notes from the previous measure to get you started in the right place and at the right tempo. Creating a "clickless" sequence is certainly not something to be attempted if you're new to sequencing, but once you get your feet wet, it's not too difficult to pull off.

Sequencing to create a live ensemble

Many small churches or church plants have very few, if any, musicians available for worship. Churches of all sizes often have studies, small groups, retreats, and other events where worship music is desired, but no musicians are available. Some churches address this need by purchasing recorded audio tracks on cassette or CD to provide accompaniment. And while these products do provide a degree of assistance, their shortcomings are also evident. Audio recordings of this type are *fixed* in that their tempo, key, and instrumentation are unable to be changed. MIDI sequences, on the other hand, are extremely flexible. With a sequence, we can change the key, the tempo, and even the instrumentation, including individual volume levels of each instrument. You can even subtract, or "mute," tracks in a sequence by temporarily removing an instrument from the mix. This is valuable if, from week to week, you're not exactly sure which musicians will be available. If your bass player shows up unexpectedly, simply mute the bass track in the sequence. If your bassist cancels at the last minute, you're still covered. Utilizing MIDI sequencing can greatly enhance the ministry value of the occasion.

This ministry snapshot story is my own. When I moved from California to help start Renaissance Church in Millburn, New Jersey, we had only a handful of people and no musicians. Yet we were committed to providing a worship experience that included modern musical styles. To make things harder, being new to the community, I didn't know any musicians. While we now have a very gifted group of musicians, our humble beginnings included two or three sequenced songs to which I'd play along on my Roland XV-88 keyboard each week. While it was a lot of work initially to create these sequences, it didn't take long to develop a nice little library of worship songs. When repeating a worship song we'd done before, we'd add variety by changing an instrument patch or changing the tempo. This would add a different flavor to the music and, as a result, keep our MIDI files fresh. As we grew and added musicians, our sequences became more supplemental in nature, which illustrates how versatile sequencing is no matter what season your ministry is in.

Cakewalk Home Studio is a simple and affordable, yet powerful sequencing program for Windows. It has music notation and audio recording capabilities, and supports virtual synthesizer and effects plug-ins.

Sequencing for rehearsals

Most church musicians have little trouble seeing the huge potential of MIDI sequencing in a worship service. But what about rehearsals? Often overlooked, sequencing can assist vocalists and instrumentalists in learning their parts, enabling them to play and sing with greater authenticity.

The music directors at Willow Creek Community Church regularly create sequences to better communicate the intended feel of an arrangement to their instrumentalists. Those same sequences are often converted to audio CDs that will become rehearsal tracks for the vocalists. This makes it possible for vocalists and instrumentalists to work on their parts on their own time, allowing them to come to rehearsal with a greater level of preparation. I imagine that some of you are salivating at that thought!

Roland's MT-300S can be best described as a MIDI boom box. It's basically a MIDI file player/sequencer with a built-in synthesizers and speakers. It's completely self-contained and even the most techno-phobic, non-musician can operate it with very little preparation or training. Although it will play any Standard MIDI File, it is especially useful for playing commercial General MIDI or GS compatible files. It can also be triggered as a sound module from a keyboard or other MIDI controller, and record sequences as well.

Don't overlook the value of MIDI sequencing when it comes to developing young or inexperienced instrumentalists. With MIDI, it's possible to create a sequence with a specific instrument removed as a practice tool. For example, I might create an audio CD that contains two versions of a sequence. The first version would include all the instruments in the arrangement. The second version might have the bass guitar part removed. The first version would allow a young, or inexperienced, bass player to hear what a good, musical bass line might sound like. The second (bassless) version would enable him or her to play along. While many church musicians will struggle to find time to create sequences for rehearsals, the truth is that even one song per month will soon result in a nice rehearsal library over time, not to mention an improved stable of musicians.

Songwriting, composing, and arranging

Those church musicians who write music for worship will find sequencing an invaluable tool for composing. Never before have songwriters, composers, and arrangers had a tool that can give them a nearly instantaneous representation of their work! And once you get the hang of sequencing, this tool can even assist in the creative process. Experimentation has never been so easy, and so fun. Those of us who write music know that taking a chance could result in something wonderful, or something quite scary and embarrassing. The problem is that, in the past, a composer or arranger might have to wait hours, days, or even weeks to actually *hear* the music that they've just written. And if they happened to land on the *scary* side of experimentation, they'd be doing it publicly with all the musicians there to share the awkward moment with them. With sequencing, we can experiment as much as we like with the door closed. We can even wear headphones! The value here is that, over time, we will begin to learn what works and what doesn't, which will help us to be better songwriters, composers, and arrangers.

Creating Printable Notation on Your Computer

The introduction of MIDI technology, advances in software development, and the affordability of personal computers have put the ability to create professional-looking musical scores in the hands of just about any church musician. While this subject might merit its own chapter, I've chosen to include it under the banner of MIDI sequencing because, to most people, sequencing and notation are joined at the hip.

Music-notation software is basically a sequencer but with a slightly different focus. While most sequencing software is designed to create great *sounding* music, scoring software is designed to create great *looking* music. Despite this obvious difference in emphasis, sequencing and notation software operate similarly, in that the user can enter music with a MIDI controller while playing to a metronome. In fact, the very same MIDI setup used for sequencing will work for scoring. Notation software usually allows the user to enter notes via mouse or even the computer keyboard (most sequencers allow this as well). Both sequencing and notation software allow notes to be edited. Notation software however, is usually very limited in terms of what kinds of MIDI messages can be edited. Like sequencing software, it's very easy to change key, tempo, or meter in notation software. Most notation software even creates transposed instrument parts automatically. If you'd like to hear the music you're writing, notation software is also set up for playback on MIDI synthesizers. In fact, each instrument part is easily routed to a different MIDI channel so it plays the appropriate patch.

It is important to note that many professional sequencing-software programs can also create printable musical scores. In the past, it was easy to distinguish between notation and sequencing software, as their features were more distinct. Today, the line between these products continues to blur. Some sequencing programs have enough power to easily create great-looking music scores that will meet the needs of many church musicians. But if your needs extend beyond basic lead sheets and piano scores, you'll probably be better off with a dedicated notation program.

Finale (*www.makemusic.com*) and Sibelius (*www.sibelius.com*) are two popular notation programs that can be operated on either a Mac or a Windows-based PC. Both companies have downloadable demo software available on their websites.

Half-truths about the benefits of notation software

Although notation software is fairly straightforward, there are a few commonly held misconceptions or half-truths that seem to be alive and well among church musicians. In order to be perfectly clear as to what this powerful tool *can* and *cannot* do for you, let's explore two popular misconceptions:

Sibelius is the scoring software of choice for Joel Endicott, music director at Light of the Hills—the campus church at Concordia University in Irvine, California. Because the worship at Concordia is a blend of traditional and contemporary, Joel needs to be able to create a variety of musical arrangements. One minute, he's writing an arrangement for a praise band; the next, he's writing a piece for piano and flute. Joel appreciates the flexibility of Sibelius, as he prefers to switch between his MIDI keyboard and his mouse and computer keyboard while entering music. According to Joel, the greatest advantage to using scoring software is the ability to change arrangements after the fact. In order to introduce variety, Joel will often rewrite the introduction or ending of a song or hymn. Sibelius gives him the ability to save multiple versions of his congregation's favorite worship music in multiple keys.

Half-truth #1: All I have to do is play a song and hit "print"

Like any half-truth, there's enough truth in a statement like this to be confusing. It is possible to simply play a song and print it. However, the important question is: *Will my music print correctly if I just play a song and hit "print"*? The answer: Probably not. To explain why this is true, we need to know a little bit about sequencing and a little bit about music notation. Earlier in this chapter we learned how a sequencer uses a click track to discern the timing of the notes we're playing. We also learned how difficult it is to play rhythmically perfect. The rub here is that the notation software doesn't know what you meant to play. It only knows what you *actually* play. For example, if you *meant* to play two half notes but were a little hasty in removing your fingers from the keyboard, you might get something like the following.

What you meant to play:

What you actually played:

If you're writing piano- or keyboard-oriented music, you may take for granted that a particular passage that hovers around middle-C is played with your right hand. However, your notation software doesn't know what you *meant*. Therefore, it tries to interpret what you played. Although there are features on most software applications that help in this regard, situations like the following still arise:

Your perception of what you played:

How your software interpreted what you played:

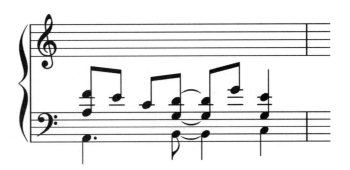

The good news is that most notation software can be configured to keep problems like these to a minimum. Also, transcription errors can be fixed on a global basis or note by note. The key point is, while notation software is extremely powerful and intuitive, it cannot read your mind. Therefore, allow some time to tweak your score after playing your parts.

 Creating a customized template is a great way to save time while writing music on a computer. The key is to create templates that fit your commonly used ensembles as well as your work style. If you commonly write for SATB (soprano, alto, tenor, bass) vocals, develop a template that already includes the appropriate staves. If you like text to appear a particular way, save your font, point size, and location preferences in the template as well. If you commonly write rhythm charts for a band, consider creating a template that includes rhythm slashes for every conceivable rhythm that you're likely to encounter. That way you can simply cut and paste, instead of having to create everything from scratch.

Half-truth #2: If I buy the right software, I can print out my music even though I don't read music well.

You *can* print music even if you don't know how to read. *But if you don't know anything about music notation, you can't expect to create scores that are musically correct.* Precisely because of the situations that arise in *Half-truth #1*, a basic knowledge of musical notation is crucial to creating readable scores. It's true that good scoring software does a lot of the work for us. But the bottom line is that scoring software is not a substitute for musical knowledge.

FIVE

PLAYING KEYBOARDS IN WORSHIP

The *keyboard* has been a recurring character in our first four chapters, but mostly as part of the supporting cast as we've been focusing on *MIDI* and *sequencing* technologies. In this chapter, it's time for the keyboard to take center stage as we discover how this very powerful instrument can enhance your worship program. We'll look at different types of electronic keyboards, and we'll learn how to choose a keyboard that meets the needs of your church. We'll also look at the role of the keyboard player in worship, as well as discover some tips on how to get the most out of your keyboard. Finally, we'll examine some often overlooked, but ever-so-vital add-ons that make your keyboard-playing experience a positive one.

:::::: A Keyboard Tour

Although dozens of new keyboards are introduced each year, most keyboards fall into one of three categories: *synthesizers*, *digital pianos*, and *workstations*. Because of the incredible versatility of today's instruments, there is a certain amount of overlap between categories. Therefore, please remember that these categories are descriptive in nature and are simply a tool to describe how certain keyboards are used. In reality, all of these keyboards are synthesizers, but in this chapter, a *synthesizer* will refer to any keyboard that is not a digital piano or a workstation.

Digital pianos

A digital piano is essentially a synthesizer designed to simulate the sound and feel of an acoustic piano. It's important to note that although a digital piano is indeed a synthesizer, it is designed for pianists, hence the name. While a digital piano may have a variety of sounds in its preset memory, the majority of patches center around pianos and other keyboard instruments, like electric pianos and organs. Since these sounds are the main focus, digital pianos tend to have a smaller number of other types of sounds. The emphasis is on authenticity and realism of the sounds as opposed to sheer quantity. In order to better simulate the experience of playing an acoustic piano, digital pianos typically have 88 keys and utilize a weighted key action. As a result, digital pianos are larger and heavier than their 61- or 76-key synthesizer counterparts. Most of today's digital pianos are multitimbral and can perform keyboard layers and splits. Despite being focused on piano sounds, some digital pianos have enough patches of other instrument types to be used for sequencing. Some digital pianos are even General MIDI or General MIDI 2 compatible, making them suitable for use with commercial Standard MIDI Files.

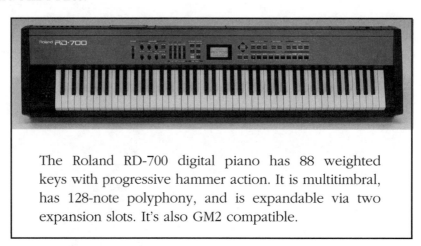

The Roland RD-700 digital piano has 88 weighted keys with progressive hammer action. It is multitimbral, has 128-note polyphony, and is expandable via two expansion slots. It's also GM2 compatible.

Because the piano has been a staple in most churches for decades, the digital piano is a natural choice for many church musicians. Most church keyboard players tend to be pianists who are most comfortable playing an 88-key, weighted keyboard. A digital piano can provide a familiar *feel* to the pianist and a familiar sound to the congregation, while at the same time adding new and different sounds and capabilities to the worship service.

Synthesizers

By now, you're probably beginning to realize that the term synthesizer can be used to describe a wide variety of instruments. While this is true, for our purposes here we will use "synthesizer" to describe those keyboards that don't fit into the digital piano or workstation categories.

Synthesizers are focused on the ability to create a very wide variety of sounds, ranging from emulations of acoustic instruments to otherworldly, electronic sounds. Synthesizers tend to have very large memory banks that can hold hundreds of patches. They also have extensive editing capabilities that allow the user to alter the sound and store the customized result for future use. Because the focus is on sonic variety, synthesizers are usually not designed to emulate the feel of an acoustic piano. Although there are exceptions, most synthesizers tend to come in either 61- or 76-key configurations. Instead of weighted-action keys, most synthesizers have non-weighted keys that are similar to traditional organ keys. It is important to note that almost all synthesizer keyboards are velocity sensitive and, as a result, can be played with a great deal of expression. Synthesizers usually have extensive MIDI capabilities, as they are often used in configurations with multiple MIDI devices. Most are also highly expandable, using various forms of expansion boards or cards (more on this later).

The Roland SRX-02 Concert Piano expansion board allows you to add 64MB of great piano sounds to your keyboard or sound module with a minimal investment. It installs easily in only a couple of minutes and can be used in any SRX-compatible synthesizer.

Workstations

We learned in Chapter Four that a *workstation* is essentially a synthesizer with a sequencer built in. What we didn't learn is that workstations come in various shapes and sizes. There are workstations that resemble digital pianos with 88 weighted-action keys. There are also workstations that have 61 or 76 non-weighted, organ-like keys. Virtually all workstations provide the ability to store sequences and sounds to some sort of removable media. This has traditionally been a floppy disk. Recently some workstations have started using smart media cards, which provide significantly more storage capacity. Workstations provide a very powerful, and highly portable, all-in-one solution for the creation of instrumental tracks that can be used in worship, rehearsal, and for songwriting or recording.

Choosing a Keyboard

When choosing a keyboard, the trick is to find an instrument that can serve you *today*. But since you don't always know what your needs will be in the future, it's good to get an *open-ended* instrument that gives you room to grow and expand. A winning strategy for choosing the right keyboard can be expressed in the following two goals: *usability* and *flexibility*.

There's nothing more frustrating than purchasing a piece of electronic equipment only to find that, because of a steep learning curve, it's going to take weeks before it will actually become useful. In order to avoid this, put *usability* as a primary goal. While this sounds like common sense, in reality it's easy to get caught up in the "wow" factor when looking at new technology and, consequently, end up with a poor choice. So how do you keep your focus on usability? The answer is to spend some time identifying your needs. Think of how you'll use the keyboard in a given month and make a list of all your needs. Ask questions like: *"What kinds of sounds are important to me?" "How many keys do I need?" "Do I want weighted keys?" "How about portability?" "A sequencer?"* But don't stop there. Divide your list into priorities. Create categories that make sense to you in order to determine which features will be deal breakers and which will be luxuries. My list typically has three levels of priorities:

- *Gotta have*—for those features that I just can't live without
- *Like to have*—for those features that would be nice, but not completely necessary
- *Doesn't matter*—for those features that have little to no value to me

Now that you've begun zeroing in on which keyboard is most *usable* from day one, it's time to shift the focus to flexibility. As important as it is to choose a keyboard that allows you to hit the ground running, you also don't want to box yourself in with a keyboard that is closed to future growth. The trouble is that sometimes the *like-to-haves* (from our priority list) become *gotta-haves* as time passes. This is why *flexibility* needs to be a primary goal as well. Here is a list of things to consider that will help you anticipate future needs:

- *Are you primarily a pianist?* If so, you'll probably be happier in the long run with an 88-key, weighted-action keyboard. If you're an organist, you may be happy with a synthesizer's fewer keys and synth-action keyboard.

- *Do you want to use MIDI sequencing in worship?* If so, you may want to consider a workstation. Even if you're planning on creating the sequence on a computer, you may want to utilize a workstation in order to play the sequence in the worship service. Otherwise, you'll need a computer or an external sequencer on hand to play the sequence during the service.

- *Do you anticipate wanting to upgrade or add new sounds at a later date?* If so, you may want to consider choosing a keyboard that is expandable. Some keyboards have expansion slots where more and/or different sounds can be added at a later date.

- *Do you like to customize things?* If you're the sort who likes to customize your computer, your office, or whatever, you might want to consider a synthesizer that has considerable editing capabilities. While you may not do much editing right from the start, it's nice to know that the potential is there as you grow.

- *Are you a visual person?* If so, you may want to shy away from keyboards with cluttered controls, opting instead for a keyboard with a large, user-friendly display.

- *Do you have friends who are more advanced than you are?* If you have keyboard-playing friends who are a couple laps ahead of you on the track, you might want to consider a keyboard from the same manufacturer as theirs. While some of the features may differ, most models from a single manufacturer operate similarly. Therefore, you'll always have personal technical support. Just make sure you reward them for their efforts!

The Role of the Keyboard Player

Keyboard instruments have long been the norm in churches. Yet, with the ever-changing world of music technology, the keyboard-player's role has never been quite so elusive. In organ-led worship, the keyboardist is song leader, accompanist, and even orchestrator simultaneously. Pianists often play the role of rhythm section in addition to accompanist. Keyboard players who play in a modern rhythm section (with drums, bass, and guitar), may be *driving the train* one minute and playing a secondary role to the other instruments the next. In the next few paragraphs, we'll take a look at the various hats that a keyboardist is asked to wear. We'll also discover some tips that will enable your "hat" to fit better—no matter which one you choose to wear!

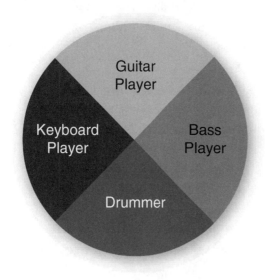

Clinicians who teach modern ensembles to play more musically as a group often refer to the *100 Percent Rule*. In this concept, the music is seen as a pie, and each instrument represents a piece of the pie. Each piece of the pie represents the amount of music that each instrument is responsible for. A keyboard player fits into that pie chart differently, depending on which hat he or she is wearing.

Soloist

If you're a soloist and no other instruments are present, then you are essentially 100 percent of our pie chart. Therefore, the responsibility to provide the melody, harmony, and rhythm is solely yours. If you're performing on a synthesizer and using layered patches, be careful, because you're playing two or more instruments now. There's still only one pie, so adjust your playing to make sure that the layers don't become muddy or cluttered. You may have to use less sustain pedal or play fewer notes depending on the patches you're layering.

Accompanist

If you are accompanying yourself or another singer, you're still 100 percent of the instrumentation. However, now you need to be more aware of how you're complementing the melody and the range of the vocalist for whom you're providing accompaniment. If you're accompanying on a synthesizer and you're layering patches, like piano and strings for example, these issues are even more important. You're not just a keyboardist: Now you're an orchestrator!

Rhythm section

A rhythm section is typically defined as a contemporary ensemble consisting of drums, bass, guitar, and possibly keyboards. In this situation, because there are four instrumentalists present, the keyboardist's share of the pie chart would be 25 percent. That means that we *share* the responsibility of providing melodic, harmonic, and rhythmic support. If each instrument plays as if it were solely responsible for all these elements, the music would sound cluttered or muddy. Unfortunately, keyboard players are often the culprits here. No other instrument in the rhythm section can play as low or as high as a keyboard. No other instrument can create thick harmonies like a keyboard. The keyboard is also the only instrument that can play extreme ranges and thick harmonic content while playing complex rhythms. While the keyboard is, indeed, a wonderful instrument, it can also do a lot of damage! This potential is even greater if you're layering patches.

Learning to play together as a team can have the same effect as purchasing a new sound system! While this may seem a bit far-fetched, it's quite true. When the individual musicians in an ensemble clutter the music by playing in non-musical ways, the result is the same kind of sonic harshness that an inferior sound system often has. Conversely, when a group of musicians learns to complement each other musically while playing together, the result is clarity of sound that often fools the listener into thinking that the church must have replaced the sound system.

So how can we as keyboard players *stay out of the way*? Here's a quick list of five suggestions:

- *Don't play octaves in your left hand if a bass player is present.* The bass player's primary role is to *anchor* the harmony by emphasizing root movement in a rhythmic partnership with the drums. While it's not wrong to play notes with your left hand, it's important to realize that in many cases low notes are not only redundant, but often clutter up the music. Bottom line: Try not to step on the bass player. He'll probably treat you much better if you don't!

- *Be aware of the rhythmic character of your patch.* If your ensemble has a number of percussive instruments, you may want to select a more sustained patch or "pad" that provides a contrast to the other instruments. Too many percussive instruments playing at once will tend to clutter the music. A sustained string patch will provide a nice canvas for the other percussive instruments to paint upon.

- *Be aware of the range of the guitar player.* Guitars and keyboards often share the same range. Therefore, if we're not careful, we can muddy the music by playing in the same limited range as the guitar player. The solution? Move up or down an octave, depending on where the guitar player isn't.

- *Play contrasting parts.* The human ear has a difficult time picking out two distinct musical parts when they're playing similar rhythms and in a similar range. However, the human ear can pick out parts quite easily if the two parts contrast in some way. Orchestrators use this philosophy while arranging for the different sections of an orchestra. If one section is playing high, sustained notes, another section might play a more rhythmic part in a lower register. The key here is contrast. If other instruments are playing longer, sustained notes with slow attacks, you might want to introduce some rhythm. If other instruments are playing in low registers, you might want to play something very high—a string obbligato, for example.

- *Keep it simple.* This well-worn slogan works well in an ensemble of any size. Remember, we're not responsible for creating 100 percent of the music. Therefore, let's keep our parts simple and allow space for the music to breathe. It might be a bit scary to try at first, but just about everyone will immediately notice the difference! Any true musician will tell you: Less is more.

As a second keyboard player

It's become increasingly common to find two keyboard players in a worship ensemble. Although there are always exceptions, most of the time one of the keyboard players is functioning as a primary keyboard player with the other as a *second keyboard player*. The *primary keyboard player* is usually functioning as a *pianist* of sorts. This keyboard player may or may not actually be playing an acoustic piano. They may, in fact, be playing a synthesizer with an electric piano patch, like a Fender Rhodes. It's not the specific instrument that's important here. Rather it's the manner in which it's being played. Pianos, as we know, are percussive in nature and a piano part generally contains a healthy amount of notes. Because we seek to create *contrast* in order to be musical, the secondary keyboard player needs to select patches that are complementary to the primary keyboard player. This would typically mean that the second keyboard player would choose patches that are not percussive but, rather, *sustained* in nature. These kinds of patches are often called pads as they essentially create a soft pad upon which the rest of the music sits. *Pads* provide the sonic glue that holds the music together. While not glamorous or flashy, pads can really provide depth and thickness to an ensemble's sound. Of course, the *100 Percent Rule* still applies when you're the second keyboard player. The rules of contrast apply as well.

Playing Pads: While pads provide thickness to the music, the chords used to play pads need not be thick. In fact, sometimes the best pads are made of one or two notes. To learn how to play pads, listen to your favorite recordings to see if you can hear a pad. *What kind of patch was used? How many notes are in each chord? What range was the pad played in?*

A great way to practice playing pads is to play two-note chords while playing a familiar chorus or hymn. Only change notes when the chord changes. Try to play notes that require as little movement as possible (voice leading) throughout the song.

⠿⠿⠿⠿ Choosing and Organizing Patches

Given that today's keyboards have hundreds of sounds available at the touch of a button, choosing an appropriate patch is not only a pleasure, but it can take some time. We all want to feel like we're getting our money's worth by playing as many different sounds as possible. But how do we find the time to listen to *every* patch? And is using different patches on every song even desirable? How do we find the right patch for the song? And how do we remember where each patch is located once we find one we like? These are valid questions.

It's an extremely good idea to audition the patches in your keyboard from time to time. In addition to listening to your keyboard's capabilities when you first purchase it, you'll find that revisiting that process on occasion will be a valuable investment of time. It's not that the sounds change—we change. We may find that we overlooked a patch a few months ago that now excites us. Revisiting your keyboard's capabilities will help avoid this.

But what do we do with the sounds we like when we find them? When auditioning patches, take some notes on a piece of paper that tell you:

1. The name of the patch

2. Where it's located (the *bank* and *patch number*)

3. A brief description of the sound

4. How you envision using it

Most experienced keyboard players keep a mental or written priority list of the types of sounds they envision using in worship. These sounds will, undoubtedly, include pianos, organs, string ensemble patches, melodic instruments, and more. It's highly likely that you'll use a piano patch more frequently than a flute patch in the context of worship. Therefore, make that part of your priority list. These are your *bread-and-butter* patches. You'll probably find that you'll have less than twenty, and possibly less than ten.

Once you've identified these patches, you need to find a way to organize them for easy access. After all, what good is a list like this if you have to scroll through dozens of patches before you find the one you're looking for. Obviously this is not a good recipe for fluidity in worship!

The key to keeping track of your bread-and-butter sounds is the *user bank* or *favorites bank*. You may recall that in addition to the factory preset patches, most synthesizers have a *user bank* for the purpose of storing custom patches. While it's true that many keyboards give us the ability to edit patches and store the customized results, we can also simply move patches from the factory presets to the user bank. Moving patches to the user bank allows us to group the sounds that we like best into easily accessible subgroups. For example, I may have three different piano sounds that I like: One might be a relatively bright sounding acoustic piano that works great for up-tempo numbers; another piano patch might be darker and warmer, suitable for slower, more introspective songs or those in which the piano is very exposed; the third piano patch might not be an acoustic piano at all but an electric piano patch. In order to keep these sounds organized, I might save these patches to numbers *one, two* and *three* in the user bank. If I commonly use organ sounds, I might want to assign my favorite organ patches nearby. I might save a pipe organ to user bank number *four*, and a Hammond-style organ to user bank number *five*. The end result is that we have all of our bread-and-butter sounds easily accessible. While it's wise to determine which patches will be played before the service starts, organizing our sounds like this allows us to make quick changes should the need arise.

Rob Rinderer leads the band from the keyboard in his duties as music director at Coast Hills Community Church in Aliso Viejo, California. A veteran musician with years of professional experience in the studio and on the stage, Rob agreed to share his thoughts on choosing sounds for worship:

"More than any other instrument, the keyboard can influence the color of the song because there are so many sound options." Therefore, Rob believes that choosing wisely is an important responsibility. "Variety can be overdone," says Rob. "What kind of piece is it? What's the emotion of the song?" These are the important questions that every keyboard player should ask, according to Rob.

Some synthesizers also have a feature called *favorites* or *favorite list*. Favorites are like bookmarks and allow you to simply "tag" a patch. Doing so assigns that patch to a particular button on the keyboard, which, when pressed, instantly calls it up. It works a lot like your Web browser software, which allows you to bookmark a certain website and create a button for it or put it in a list that you can access quickly.

Finally, *how do we decide which patches to choose?* While there a few helpful hints to consider, it really does come down to your own personal preference. This is where artistry enters the picture. What kind of feeling are you trying to convey? What are the lyrics about? Choose a sound that would best convey that sentiment. As for the helpful hints, consider the following:

- *Consider what role you're playing before you consider what sound to play.* If you're the only instrumentalist present, you'll most likely want to consider playing a piano-type sound. You may have a great sounding string ensemble patch. But a long, sustained patch is not likely to provide enough rhythmic motion to lead most congregations. If there's a pianist and you're the second keyboard player, then don't choose a piano-type sound (no matter how good your keyboard sounds). Choose something that will be appropriate for your ensemble.

- *Consider your congregation before you consider what sound to play.* In a traditional congregation, it's probably not wise to play a majority of patches that have an electronic sound to them. In a traditional context, it's wise to consider introducing new technology through familiar means. This might mean a pipe organ, or possibly, an acoustic piano. If you have to satisfy your "rebellious desires," layer it with a soft string pad.

- *Consider your ensemble before you consider what sound to play.* Don't choose sounds that are too similar to other instruments in your ensemble. For example, if you have an electric guitar player, it's probably not a good choice to select an electric guitar patch. It would be redundant and probably result in cluttering the music.

Playing with Integrity

Because today's keyboards can emulate acoustic instruments with astonishing authenticity, it's easy to assume that we can create convincing renditions of guitars, strings, brass, and other familiar instruments simply by choosing the right patch. This is only half true. In order to truly emulate an acoustic instrument, it's crucial that we learn to play in a manner that's consistent with how the original instrument is played. For example, a trumpet patch played an octave below middle-C is no longer a trumpet. A French horn part that contains nothing but up-tempo sixteenth notes is less than authentic as well. Experienced keyboard players are like spontaneous orchestrators, in that they're able to play in a manner that is both authentic and very convincing. In fact, you'll find that the same patch that achieves a high level of realism can also sound cheap and fake, depending on who is playing it. In the same way, it's not uncommon for a mediocre synthesizer to sound great when played appropriately by an accomplished keyboardist. Besides studying orchestration, a great way to learn to play with increasing authenticity is to listen to a variety of instruments, making note of their tonal characteristics and how they're played. *What is the range? Is this a slow-speaking instrument or an instrument that can be played very fast? Is this a percussive instrument, or is it usually played in a sustained manner? Is this instrument usually played melodically or part of a harmonic section? Where does this instrument usually fit in an orchestration?* Investing some time and effort into becoming a spontaneous orchestrator will pay off in powerful ways as you bring a new level of musical integrity to your worship as a keyboard player.

Keyboard Accessories You Don't Want to Forget

With the amazing capabilities found in keyboard technology, it's easy to forget about some of the less-glamorous accessories that make keyboard playing a pleasant experience. Some of these accessories are simple accessories that provide functionality to the keyboard. Others are powerful add-ons that add features, sounds, or other kinds of capabilities. We'll look at the most commonly used accessories or add-ons used in a worship context:

Keyboard stand

Many keyboards suitable for use in a worship environment do not come with a stand. Therefore, you'll need to purchase one. Whether you're buying your first stand or looking to replace an existing one, here are some things to consider when buying a keyboard stand:

- *How many keyboards will you use?* Some stands provide the ability to utilize more than one keyboard at a time, while others are designed for a single keyboard. Even if you use a single keyboard, you might want to consider a multi-tiered keyboard stand if you think there's a chance you'll move in that direction in the future. Some stands are expandable, so you can start with one tier and add another later should the need arise.

- *How big is your keyboard?* If you have a rather large keyboard with 88 keys, you'll want to find a stand that is sturdy enough to provide the amount of stability you're comfortable with.

- *How portable do you need to be?* The most heavy-duty stands that provide a great amount of stability tend to be large, heavy objects themselves. As a result, they're also less portable. You'll want to think this through before making your choice. Your back will thank you for it!

Keyboard Case

In order to protect your investment, you'll want to have a case for your keyboard. Like keyboard stands, there are a wide variety of models available. With cases, a general rule of thumb is: The stronger the protection, the heavier it will be and the weaker the protection, the lighter it will be. Once again, you'll need to determine how portable you need your keyboard to be. If you're looking at one or two local moves per year, then a softer, lighter case can be used. But if you're looking at a lot of moves, or even the possibility of transporting by airline, a hard-shell case is necessary. Whichever case you determine is best for your needs, it's highly recommended that you find a case that is made for your particular size or model of keyboard—a better fit equals better protection.

Hold pedal

Many keyboards do not come with a hold pedal included. Some hold pedals are inexpensive, little square pedals. While in most cases, this type of pedal will do nicely, some hold pedals are designed to look and feel like a piano's sustain pedal, and may even include an anti-slip feature that keeps the pedal firmly in place on the floor.

Expression pedal

An expression pedal is a real-time controller that can be used for a variety of performance features. An expression pedal can control volume, modulation, stereo panning, or any number of other features. Many keyboards allow more than one expression pedal to be used at once. An expression pedal can even control one patch while leaving another unchanged. This is an extremely powerful way to use layers in a worship set-

The Roland EV-5 Expression Pedal can be assigned to control a variety of performance functions.

ting. For example, in a layer of piano and strings, the expression pedal can be used to fade the strings in and out without affecting the volume of the piano!

Expansion boards

Many keyboards are built to allow the addition of an *expansion board* in order to add more sounds to the keyboard's built-in library. Expansion boards are often thematically packaged; that is, they include sounds from a specific instrument group or genre of music. Expansion boards usually come in the form of a small circuit board that can easily be installed by virtually anyone. Adding an expansion board is a great (and inexpensive) way to update an older keyboard with newer technology.

SIX

GUITAR
TECHNOLOGY
IN WORSHIP

At first glance, guitar technology may seem more straight-forward than keyboard technology. After all, there are only a handful of variations: acoustic or electric, steel strings or nylon strings, and six strings or twelve. Yet it doesn't take much exploration to discover that today's guitar technology rivals the keyboard in terms of variety of sounds and performance capabilities. And yet, like keyboard technology, these new tools are more affordable and easier to use than ever before. In this chapter, we'll learn all about:

- Guitar types and their applications for worship
- Guitar amps in a worship setting
- Guitar processing
- Guitar synthesizers
- Modeling technology for guitars
- Choosing sounds in a worship context
- Choosing equipment for a worship setting

We'll also hear how two guitar players use guitar technology to enhance the worship ministry of their congregations.

Guitar Types and Their Applications for Worship

Most people are familiar with common types of guitars: electric, acoustic, six-string, twelve-string, nylon-string, and steel-string. These are all descriptive terms that most likely bring an image to mind while reading. However, each guitar type contains subtle variations within its family, as well as unique capabilities and challenges. For our purposes, we'll separate these guitars into two families: *acoustic* and *electric*.

Acoustic guitars

These guitars all share the ability to create sound without amplification (though they most certainly can be amplified). Acoustic guitars differ in the following ways:

- *Number of strings:* Although most acoustic guitars used in worship are six-string models, some guitarists prefer to use twelve-string models. The six-string acoustic guitar tends to be more versatile and can be used in a variety of settings for a variety of styles. Twelve-string models provide a bigger sound, and because of their tuning, create a distinctive tone.

- *String type:* Acoustic guitars typically used in worship have either steel strings or nylon strings. Nylon-string guitars are often referred to as *classical guitars*, as they are commonly used for classical music. Steel-string guitars tend to have a brighter, louder sound while nylon-string guitars tend to have a softer, mellower sound.

- *Body type:* Acoustic guitars are also available in several different sizes. Although there is a great deal of complexity involved in their design and construction, larger body types tend to be louder and have more *bottom* to the sound, while smaller body types tend to be brighter and produce less sound. Steel-string guitars are available in a variety of body types. The most common body style is called the *dread-nought*. This body style has been around for nearly a hundred years and is highly versatile. Slightly larger than the dreadnought is the *jumbo*. The jumbo, because of its width, allows for the deepest tone of the various body types. Smaller than the dreadnought are the *grand auditorium* and *grand concert* body types. These body types are popular choices for guitarists who regularly play through an amplifier or sound system because these body styles reduce the potential for feedback. Smallest of the body styles is the *classical* guitar. This body shape is designed for use with nylon strings. Finally, regardless of the number or type of strings, many acoustic guitars have *cutaways*. A cutaway is simply an alteration of the body that gives the player access to the highest frets on the neck of the guitar.

Another important area of acoustic-guitar technology that we need to discuss is *amplification*. Although an acoustic guitar may provide enough sound for worship in a small setting, most congregations will find that an acoustic guitar is simply not able to produce enough volume to fill a large room or compete with the volumes of other instruments. Therefore, the sound must be amplified in some way. Some players use amplifiers designed specifically for acoustic guitars (more on these later). However, most guitarists and sound technicians choose to amplify the acoustic guitar through the main sound system. This can be accomplished by using a *microphone* or, more commonly, a *pickup*.

While microphones would provide the best sound quality in a perfect world, there are several variables that make microphones a less desirable choice in the real world. Microphones do a fantastic job of capturing the complex sound of an acoustic guitar. The problem, however, is that a microphone placed in front of an acoustic guitar will also capture other sounds in the vicinity. Therefore, it will not only amplify the guitar, but also the congregation, as well as any other instrument or voice that is nearby. The end result is an undefined, cluttered sound that most of us would rather not have in a worship setting.

The preferred method for amplifying acoustic guitars is through the use of a *pickup*. A pickup typically comes in one of two forms. A sound-hole pickup, also called an *electromagnetic pickup*, is a device that fits into the sound hole of the guitar. It works by detecting the motion of the strings and converting it into a usable signal that can be fed into a sound system for amplification. Another common type of pickup is called a *contact pickup*. Also called a *piezo pickup*, this type of pickup makes contact with a part of the guitar (usually under the saddle) and converts vibrations into an electrical signal. This signal can be fed into a sound system for amplification. The piezo pickup offers a high-quality amplified sound with a low risk of feedback, and it's relatively inexpensive, making it the most common among acoustic guitar players in a worship setting.

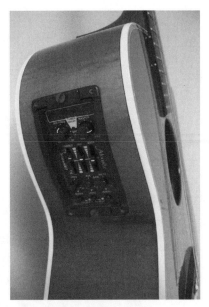

It's also important to note that there are several *hybrid pickups* that combine both a microphone and a piezo pickup in order to reproduce an acoustic guitar's sound. The microphone is usually permanently installed in the body of the guitar (often at the factory), with the piezo pickup installed under the saddle. These hybrid pickups typically also include a *preamp* that allows the player to blend between the microphone and the pickup.

Preamp and equalizer for a piezo pickup

The AD-3 Acoustic Instrument Processor from BOSS is a footswitch controlled effects processor made for acoustic guitar that provides digital reverb, digital chorus, EQ, and an anti-feedback function.

Electric guitars

Unlike their acoustic counterparts, *electric guitars* require an amplifier to be heard. It can be said that electric guitars were originally intended simply to be *louder acoustic guitars*. However, with the addition of amplifiers, processors, and even synthesizers, today's electric guitar sound palette is limited only by one's imagination. Electric guitars commonly found in worship are almost always six-string models (although twelve-string models do exist). Electric guitars utilize steel strings and rely on a pickup to create their sound. While electric guitars share many similarities, there are some differences as well. They include:

- *Body type*: There are two main body styles and a great number of hybrid variations on these themes. The two body types are *hollow body* and *solid body*. The hollow body guitar is just what it sounds like: a hollow-bodied guitar. This guitar is similar to an acoustic guitar in that it can create sound on its own, although it's not designed to be played without an amplifier. Some hollow bodies have *f-holes* in the top. Others have completely solid tops with no sound holes of any kind. A hollow-body electric guitar typically has a warm, round sound that is often associated with traditional jazz, although it can be used in other styles. A solid-body

The Fender Stratocaster is a popular solid-body electric guitar

guitar is what its name suggests: a guitar whose body is made from a solid piece of wood. These guitars make very little sound when played without amplification. While the size, shape, and type of wood are factors in the sound, solid-body guitars, when amplified, have a brighter, and perhaps more versatile-sound that can be shaped in a variety of ways by the configuration of the pickups.

- *Pickup type and configuration:* Electric guitars generally have two or three pickups built into the body of the guitar. Besides the body type, there are two key factors in shaping the tone of an electric guitar: the *type of pickup* and the *location* or *configuration of the pickups.* There are two types of pickups: *single coil* and *double coil,* which are also called *humbucking* pickups. Single-coil pickups tend to be brighter sounding while double-coil pickups tend to be warmer sounding. Pickup placement is equally important to the character of the sound. A pickup that is close to the bridge (where the strings originate near the bottom of the guitar) will tend to be brighter and thinner. A pickup placed near the

A guitar with humbucker pickups

neck of the guitar will be warmer and richer. A popular pickup configuration found in modern electric guitars contains a double-coil pickup near the bridge and two single-coil pickups near the neck. This arrangement provides the player with the best of both worlds.

Guitar Amplifiers in a Worship Setting

To many church music directors, guitar amplifiers seem like a necessary evil. Truly, electric guitars can't be heard without them, so amplifiers are a necessity. Yet many guitarists have trouble creating a usable sound without turning the volume up beyond an acceptable level. This can create disharmony among the other instrumentalists, as well as within the congregation. In this section, we'll attempt to demystify the process of getting great sounds out of the guitar while preserving the peace!

The purpose of a guitar amplifier is simple—to enable an electric guitar to be heard at the proper volume level. But guitar amplifiers also play a role in shaping the sound of the guitar. In fact, *the guitar, the amplifier,* and the *effects processor* all participate in a partnership of sorts that collectively creates the overall guitar sound. Right now, we'll focus on each component separately, but in the real world, they're virtually inseparable.

Guitar amplifiers

Guitar amplifiers are available in various shapes, sizes, and price points. We'll focus on three things that most guitar amps share:

- *Clean channel:* Guitar amplifiers can route the incoming signal from the electric guitar to one of two channels. In the clean channel, the signal is amplified without altering the sound. Therefore, the sound is said to be "clean." This is a common choice for slower, more mellow songs where a heavy guitar sound isn't needed.

- *Distortion* or *"crunch" channel:* Usually activated with a foot switch, the incoming signal from the electric guitar can be routed to a *crunch channel.* This channel has the ability to add distortion to the incoming signal in varying degrees, which are controlled with a knob on the front panel of the amplifier. The resulting sound is typically identified as a *rock sound.* "Power chords" and lead guitar solos with sustained notes commonly use this type of sound.

- *Tone controls:* Regardless of which channel is being used, most guitar amplifiers have the ability to further shape the sound by adjusting the tone. Shaping the tone is usually accomplished by adjusting two or three knobs (depending on the model) on the front panel of the amplifier. These knobs control the *bass, treble,* and sometimes *mid-range* frequencies of the sound.

The Roland JC-120 Combo Amp

Some amps combine the amplifier electronics with one or more speakers in a single device. This configuration is called a *combo* amp. Other systems separate these components into two pieces: the *amplifier,* also called the *amp head,* and an external speaker cabinet, which houses the speaker(s). Although both configurations are found in worship settings, the combo is the more popular of the two, due to its ease of setup and transport.

Guitar Effects Processing

We've covered how the body styles and pickups of a guitar influence the character of the sound. We've also discovered how guitar amplifiers further shape that sound. The *guitar-effects processor* is the third party in this vital partnership. An effects processor is a device that creates any number of sound-altering effects. Guitar-effects processors have many shapes, sizes, and varying capabilities. The most basic type of guitar effects are found in small foot pedals, often called

The BOSS DD-6
Digital Delay effects pedal

stomp boxes. A stomp box allows the user to activate a single effect by simply stepping on a pedal. There are also more elaborate devices that can generate multiple effects simultaneously. These devices allow the guitarist to combine several effects and thus create a variety of different sounds. Like *patches* on a synthesizer, these effects combinations can be customized and saved, allowing guitarists to instantly access a certain sound by simply pressing a foot switch. These devices are either mounted in a rack and controlled by foot pedals or built into the foot pedals themselves. Here are some descriptions of commonly used effects:

- *Overdrive and Distortion:* These are similar in that they're meant to simulate the crunch or distortion channel of an amplifier. The amount and type of distortion can be adjusted on the pedal.

- *Chorus:* The original signal is mixed with a slightly detuned signal to create a *fat, rich* sound. Both electric and acoustic guitars use *chorus* effects to provide more depth to their sound. Chorus can be used in a variety of ways, but a common application is to use it with the "clean" channel.

Original sound

Chorused

- *Delay:* This is a type of "echo" effect. The amount of time before the echo begins is adjustable, as is the volume of the echoes ("taps") and the number of them. A short delay time (such as 50 milliseconds) at a healthy volume provides a thickening of the sound that simulates two guitar players playing the same part in unison. A longer delay time with a barely audible volume can provide a special effect that simulates playing in a large hall. Many delay effects devices allow the user to manually set the delay time to be in sync with the tempo of the song.

Original sound

With delay

- *Reverb:* This is a spatial effect that simulates the acoustic qualities of a room, hall, cathedral, etc. With reverb, it's possible to simulate the sound of a guitar being played in a bathroom or in a stadium—and everything in between. If your worship setting is a classroom or outdoors, a little reverb would be a nice touch. If you're in a very ambient space, like a gymnasium or any other large venue with lots of *reflective* surfaces (wood, glass, metal, etc.), you may not need any reverb—it's going to be there already.

Original sound

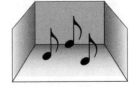
With reverb

- *Compression:* This effect controls the dynamics of the instrument. A compressor makes loud passages softer and soft passages louder. This essentially flattens out the signal and enables the guitar to sustain notes longer. Guitar players often use this effect along with distortion to "smooth out" the sound and make long note values easier to play.

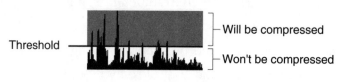

There are many other guitar effects available, as well as some variations of the effects explained above. However, the effects we've explored here are those most commonly used in a worship setting. It's important to understand that a guitar player's sound is the combined result of the pickups, the amplifier, and the effects. Each component can change the overall sound significantly or subtly, depending on the settings and adjustments that a guitarist makes while playing.

Simple and Subtle: These are the operative words for those who are new to guitar effects. The purpose of effects is to enhance the music, not overwhelm it. A good rule of thumb is that if you can hear the effect while playing with an ensemble, the effect is probably too loud. A tasteful effect will add a subtle character to the sound without giving away its identity. Once again, less *is* more.

Guitar Synthesizers

A guitar synthesizer, as the name suggests, is a synthesizer that is controlled by a guitar. The concept is very similar to a keyboard acting as a *controller*, triggering a sound module via MIDI. The difference being that the *controller* here is a *guitar.* While there are special guitars made specifically for this purpose, virtually any steel-string guitar can be fitted with a special pickup for this purpose. A guitar synthesizer can play any patch that a keyboard can play. It can even play your keyboard via MIDI! In fact, because a guitar synthesizer is MIDI capable, the entire world of MIDI is open to the guitar player! This includes sequencing, notation, layers, splits, velocity switching, and anything that a keyboard synthesizer can do.

In a worship setting, a guitar synthesizer can function as a melodic instrument—in fact, any melodic instrument! A guitar can be a flute, a trumpet, an oboe, anything you can imagine. Guitar synthesizers in a worship context also typically cover a lot of the same ground a second keyboard player would. It's common to use a guitar synthesizer for string ensemble parts or pads that enrich the sound of the ensemble. It's even possible to designate the bottom three strings for one patch and the top three strings for a different patch. The possibilities are endless.

An electric guitar with a built-in guitar synth pickup

Jimmy Leahey plays guitar at my church, Renaissance Church in Millburn, New Jersey. Although Jimmy has traditionally preferred a very basic setup with a vintage-style amplifier, he's recently branched out into the world of guitar synthesizers. When the need arises, Jimmy provides a tonal color to the worship music through his Roland GR-33 guitar synthesizer. On any given Sunday, we may need an extra keyboard part, but not have an extra keyboard player. No problem. Jimmy can add strings, horns, or anything else we might need to enhance the musical arrangement. He can even blend in his own, more traditional, guitar sound with the synthesizer patches while he plays. Jimmy's guitar synthesizer has added a whole new dimension to our musical palette!

Ministry Applications

Did you know that there are probably guitar players hiding in your congregation? Maybe they aren't skilled enough to be the main guitarist in your band, but chances are, with a little training and practice, they could add a lot to the music and perhaps even more to your ministry. Most guitar players can strum a simple chord and hold it for a measure, and that's all it takes to add a lush string section or warm pad to the arrangement using a guitar synthesizer. Even if you don't normally use a guitar in your worship, a guitar synth can supplement your style of music and support any instrumentation. It's a great way to fill out the sound and also great for your ministry.

 Here are some tips for integrating guitar technology into your worship ministry.

- *Build your ministry from within your congregation.* Find those folks in your church who sit there each week thinking, "I'd love to serve on the worship team, but I'm not good enough to be up there." Host a worship ministry outreach brunch and put an announcement in the bulletin: "If you can play ten chords on the guitar and have a heart to serve, there may be a place for you in our worship ministry."

- *Empower people and build them up in their giftedness.* Some of the most passionate worshippers in your congregation may not be the most accomplished musicians. But, with a little training, they can make a big impact on your ministry—and not just in their contribution to the music. More significantly, their attitude and heart will be a powerful example to the more accomplished musicians and can raise the spiritual "bar" in your ministry.

- *Bless your congregation.* When a congregation sees one of their own on your team, they immediately identify and respond. It's amazing how quickly the "worship watchers" in your congregation can become engaged when they see their friends participating. And don't be surprised at how fast your ministry will grow, as people who've been inspired by the investment you've made in one person, suddenly want to serve.

- *Provide a training ground for younger musicians.* Musicians who are early in their development are often excluded from ministry opportunities. Why not use that burgeoning junior high student in a support role? By the time he's ready to lead musically, he'll have benefited from your mentorship and values, making him a valuable part of your ministry that you can plug into any number of situations.

- *Leverage the instrumentalists you already have.* Sometimes a music minister is faced with having too many guitarists and not enough other instrumentalists—like keyboardists or bassists. Since a guitar synth can cover virtually any part, it makes a great substitute for the missing pieces in your ensemble. For example, if you're struggling to find a solid bass player and you have two good guitarists, simply put one on guitar synth. The guitar synth instantly transforms a guitar into a six-string bass of any variety—fretless, acoustic upright, electric, synth bass. Think outside the band.

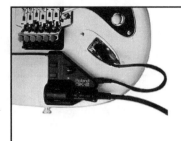

The Roland GK-2AH divided pickup is easily mounted on any acoustic or electric guitar with steel strings and can be used with Roland guitar synthesizers, modeling processors, and amplifiers.

Modeling Technology for Guitars

One of the most exciting technologies to come on the scene in recent years is *acoustic modeling*. Unlike digital-sampling technology, which uses a recorded *sample* of an acoustic instrument to create sound, acoustic modeling uses a very fast computer processor to create a *model* of an instrument, amplifier or processor, which responds in real time to the nuances in a musician's performance. This grants the musician an unprecedented amount of expression and realism.

The most successful use for acoustic modeling to date has been in the area of guitar amplifiers and processors. These amps and processors use *modeling* to create the sound of vintage amplifiers, popular guitars, even pickup configurations—all from the input of a guitar cable.

The Roland VGA-7 is a modeling amplifier that contains over 20 different amplifier models and speaker cabinet simulations. The VGA-7 also models over 26 guitar types and contains four independent effects processors. The VGA-7 has two 12" speakers and is compatible with any steel-string guitar using the GK-2AH pickup.

Some guitar-modeling amplifiers and processors use a special pickup to control the modeling effects. Although some guitar manufacturers build guitars with this pickup built in, just about any steel string-guitar can easily be outfitted for this purpose. Other modeling amplifiers and processors are able to use the signal from just about any guitar. While the technology behind modeling amplifiers and stand-alone processors is similar, there are some differences as well.

Modeling amplifiers look like conventional guitar amplifiers and are primarily designed to emulate the sound of various well-known modern and vintage amplifiers. Modeling amps come in various speaker configurations and are able to provide a

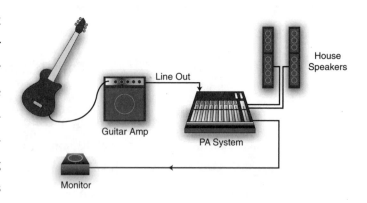

A guitar amp being used as a processor

variety of sounds at any volume. Many vintage amplifiers sound best tonally when played at a loud volume. A modeling amplifier, however, can emulate this sound, but at a volume much better suited for a worship environment. This is part of the appeal for churches! Also, modeling guitar amplifiers give the player the ability to turn the speaker off altogether, instead connecting the output jack of the amplifier to the main sound system. This gives the sound engineer the ability to control the volume level of the guitar in the service—a luxury that's not possible using a conventional guitar amp. It's also common to find various guitar effects (delay, chorus, etc.) built into modeling guitar amps. This provides a degree of overlap with *modeling processors*. The distinction here is that modeling amps are both real *amplifiers* and *effects processors*.

Modeling processors share several things in common with modeling amps. Like modeling amps, they have the ability to model the sound of various kinds of guitar amplifiers. But, they are not amplifiers in themselves—that is, they

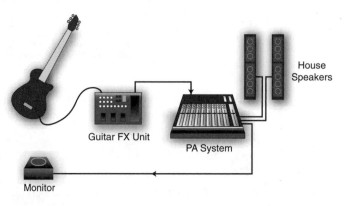

A "direct" configuration using an effects processor

have no amplifier, no speakers, and make no sound without a sound system. Modeling processors specialize in shaping the sound of the guitar through various *models* of amplifiers, speakers, and effects. The guitar player can amplify the sound of the processor in a couple of different ways: through a conventional guitar amplifier, or "direct" through the main sound system. One key advantage of a modeling processor is that the guitar player doesn't need to replace an existing amplifier to get new and different sounds. Also, if a guitar runs through a processor directly into the main sound system, the sound engineer can, once again, control the stage volume of the guitar. This is an excellent way to achieve great guitar tone without sacrificing the mix.

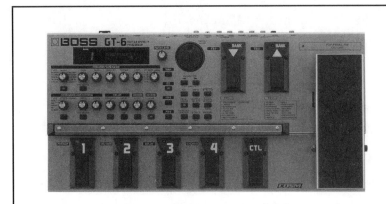

The BOSS GT-6 is a *modeling processor* for guitar. It has 30 amplifier models as well as a variety of other common guitar effects and does not need to be used with a special pickup. It's built into a foot-controllable unit that can store 340 different program settings!

Understanding and embracing the role of the guitar player in worship

Like keyboard technology, advances in guitar technology have put an unprecedented amount of possibility in the hands of the guitar player. With this capability comes the ability to enhance worship or to detract from it. In Chapter Five, we learned about the *100 Percent Rule*. This rule compares music to a pie chart, where each instrument represents a piece of the pie and is only allowed an equal share of

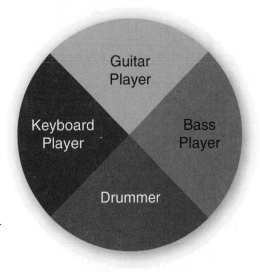

the sound. In other words, the role of each instrument is directly related to who else is playing. When no one else is playing, the guitar player *is* the band. The melody needs to be supported, the harmony needs to be defined through playing the right chords, and the tempo and groove need to be established rhythmically. When the guitar is part of a rhythm section (drums, bass, and keyboards), it doesn't need to carry the same load. If there are two guitars present, the load is even less.

Now that we better understand the role of the guitar player, we can learn to embrace it. Playing in a worship ensemble is not about individual achievement or glory; it's about unity and submission to the goal of the group—*to facilitate worship for your congregation.* The more transparent the ensemble is, the better. We want people to enjoy our music—there's nothing wrong with that. But we don't want to make the music the object of worship. In order to truly understand and embrace the guitarist's role, we need to start from here.

So how should we play? Just give the music what it needs—no more, but no less. Ask yourself: "How much rhythm does the song need in order to have momentum? What kind of sound will enhance the song without overwhelming it? Can I hear the other instruments? What can I do to complement the other instrument parts?" Any guitar player that is honestly asking these kinds of questions will become a valuable asset to any worship ensemble—musically and spiritually!

Choosing and organizing your sounds

In answering the preceding questions, we must evaluate the relationship between the *sound* of the instrument and the actual *part*, or notes, that are being played. In the same way that we want the parts we play to complement the parts being played by the other musicians, we need to make sure our sounds fit as well. For example, if the keyboard player is playing a percussive patch, like a marimba, the guitarist may not want to choose an equally percussive sound. If the keyboard player is playing something soft and lush, like a string pad, the guitarist may want to complement that sound with a brighter sound. The key issue here is that we need to listen to the other musicians to determine what sound will work best.

Because guitar players now have access to a large library of sounds, like keyboard players, the need arises to organize sounds for easy access. In Chapter Five, keyboard players were encouraged to organize their bread-and-butter sounds into similar groups and store them consecutively. Guitar players can benefit from the same advice. Most guitar players will find that they need several versions of a distorted sound and several versions of a clean sound. These variations of *clean* and *crunch* sounds may have to do with the degree of distortion, but also the other effects that are used. Most modeling amps and processors allow the user to save not only the amplifier settings, but also the effect settings in a single program. In other words, program #1 might be a slightly *distorted* sound that is *compressed* and has a barely audible *delay*. Program #2 might be the same sound without the distortion. With a little time, any guitar player can have a library of sounds that will fit any need that may arise. The possibilities are endless!

Amplifiers aren't just for *electric* guitars. The AC-100 from Roland is a small combo amp designed specifically for acoustic guitars. This is suitable for small venues like a coffeehouse, or it can be mic'd on stage while also acting as a guitar monitor. The AC-100 includes onboard EQ with a *feedback eliminator* as well as *chorus* and *digital reverb* effects to further shape the sound.

Choosing guitar equipment for a worship setting

As discussed in the previous chapter, it's vitally important to identify your needs and priorities before choosing equipment for any instrument. If you take an honest look at those needs, you'll choose wisely every time! While this is good advice, it's also generic advice. Here are some things to consider that are specific to guitar players:

- *Amplifier and/or processor?* What kind of guitar sound are you trying to create? Do you play mostly rock styles, that gravitate toward a *crunch* sound? Or will you play mostly clean sounds, or both? These are the relevant questions in making a decision about an amplifier and/or processor. If you already have an amp but would like to add some great effects to your sound, you might want to consider adding a processor to your existing amplifier. If you are attracted to having an all-in-one package, a modeling amplifier might be the best choice. Each of these products have very compelling features that will likely *knock your socks off* while standing in a music store! The key here is to identify your needs *beforehand* so that you can choose wisely and not get taken in with what has the greatest "wow" factor at the music store.

- *Amplifier size:* When guitar amplifiers were first being developed, it was common practice that only the vocals would be put through the P.A. system. Therefore, guitar players needed guitar amps loud enough to play over the rest of the band. Loud guitar amps became part of the electric guitar heritage. More and more today, guitar players are looking for amplifiers that allow them to sound great at a low volume. In a worship context, only a small amplifier is needed. When choosing an amplifier for worship, be aware of your volume constraints. Is your worship space very *live* acoustically? What is the typical volume level for your worship ensemble? Don't just choose the biggest amplifier you can afford. Most small amplifiers can play louder than you'd probably want them to. Modeling amplifiers can be a great solution for churches, as many of them have direct outputs that allow you to feed the signal straight to the main sound system—with or without the amplifier speaker on. This allows a great deal of control over the guitar player's volume in worship. In this scenario, the guitarist would hear himself/herself through a stage monitor (see diagrams on pg. 90).

- *Versatility:* What kinds of styles will be played on your amplifier or processor? If this is for the church, how many different players will use this equipment? Not only do we need to find tools that sound good, we need them to be as versatile as we are. Some amplifiers do one or two sounds extremely well but fall off a bit after that. Some processors are the same way. The key here is finding a mix of tools that meets your stylistic needs. The obvious solution is to find a single product that meets *all* your needs. But that isn't the only way, especially if you already have an amp or processor and don't want to replace it. Let's say you love your existing amplifier, but it only does *clean* sounds well. The solution would be to find a processor that has the effects you're looking for, thus providing a great complement to your existing amp. Of course, it works the other way as well. You can choose an amp that complements your favorite processor. Sometimes adding versatility is as simple and inexpensive as adding a single effects pedal. It all comes down to your needs, as well as your personal taste.

Brian Swerdfeger plays guitar in the worship band at Friends Church in Yorba Linda, California. But he's no ordinary guitar player. Brian designs and builds guitar rigs for some of the music industry's most famous guitar players. He also lends his expertise to a variety of manufacturers, helping them design and develop powerful guitar technology for the future. When I need advice on guitars, Brian is my first call. Here are a few thoughts from Brian on guitar technology in worship.

When choosing sounds for worship, Brian encourages guitar players to think like an arranger. "Today's tools for guitar can create a wider variety of sounds than ever before. Therefore, guitarists need to choose wisely when selecting what sound they'll be using. 'Does it complement the keyboard player? Does it fit with the style or message of the song?' These are the questions I encourage guitar players to ask."

"Also, there's a vital relationship between the sound and the part (notes you're playing). These elements should be inseparable," Brian says. "*The sound determines the part, and the part requires the sound.*"

On choosing the size of the amplifier for worship, Brian points out that "the amplifier volume is best when it's heard only right where the guitar player is standing. It doesn't need to be heard all over the platform!"

Brian also emphasizes the partnership that exists between each link in the guitar audio chain: the *guitar*, the *processor*, and the *amplifier*. These elements are inseparable. Brian breaks down the modern electric guitar sound into four basic categories (which are essentially subcategories of our *clean* and *crunch* categories). These four basic sounds consist of the following:

- *Clean sound*
- *Pushed clean sound* (clean tone that's slightly "dirty or dingy," as Brian puts it)
- *Crunch sound*
- *Solo tone* (high-gain crunch tone that's also compressed)

When choosing an amplifier for worship, Brian encourages guitar players to find an amp that does any two of these basic sounds well. The goal then is to find a processor that does the other two well. Remember, these pieces of equipment form a partnership (along with the guitar) to create a single sound. Brian's key recommendation is to look at a guitar rig as a single entity—not different pieces of gear.

***

While our style preferences and worship settings may differ, we can undoubtedly agree that today's guitar technology has opened the door to a whole new world for guitar players in worship.

SEVEN

BASS
TECHNOLOGY
IN WORSHIP

As contemporary styles of music have become common-place in worship, the bass is no longer only found in a string section. In fact, it's become an inseparable part of the modern praise band rhythm section. In this chapter, we'll look at various types of basses and identify common technologies that can enhance their sound. We'll also hear from a worship leader who leads from the bass.

Types of Basses

The various types of basses are determined by the following criteria:

- Electric or acoustic
- The number of strings
- Fretted or fretless

Electric or acoustic

All basses are derived from the acoustic bass known as a *string bass, upright bass, double bass,* or even *bass fiddle.* These colorful terms describe its stature as well as its shape. This instrument has traditionally found a home in an orchestral setting, but in the twentieth century, it became a staple in jazz ensembles. The string bass has four strings that are tuned one octave lower than the lowest four strings on a guitar (E-A-D-G). The electric bass came into existence shortly after the electric guitar achieved popularity. These early electric basses had four strings and were tuned to the same notes and intervals as the string bass. Electric basses require an amplifier or sound system to be heard. They use electromagnetic pickups similar to those of electric guitars. Pickup position influences the sound in the same way that it influences an electric guitar's sound. Pickups placed closest to the neck give the bass a round, warm sound, while pickups placed closest to the bridge give the bass a brighter sound.

Today, there is also the hybrid *acoustic-electric bass.* This instrument has a body shape and composition similar to a large acoustic guitar, but it uses bass strings. Although an acoustic-electric bass does create an acoustic sound on its own, this instrument generally comes with a *piezo* pickup, similar to those used on acoustic guitars.

The vast majority of basses used in worship today are electric. Therefore, we will focus mainly on technology that supports this instrument. It is important to note, however, that acoustic basses can benefit from some of the technology that we'll explore here.

The number of strings

Electric basses have evolved beyond the original four-string bass to include models with additional strings—some as many as eight. However, the most commonly used basses in a worship setting are four-string, five-string, and six-string models. Let's take a brief look at each:

- *Four-string electric bass:* This instrument has four strings, which are tuned an octave below the lowest four strings of a guitar (E-A-D-G).

- *Five-string electric bass:* This instrument simply adds a low B-string to the four-string model expanding the lower range of the instrument.

- *Six-string electric bass:* In addition to the low B-string added by the *five-string bass*, the *six-string* adds a high C-string. This provides the player with an extended upper range suitable for melodic playing.

For those just beginning to learn the electric bass, it's advisable to start on a four-string model as the larger models are a bit harder to play.

Fretted or Fretless

The other distinguishing factor among electric basses is whether or not the instrument uses frets to determine pitch. The acoustic *string bass* is a *fretless* instrument and, like its string family siblings, relies on the player's sense of intonation to play a note properly in tune. Electric *fretless basses* were introduced to provide an electric instrument that could sound similar to an acoustic string bass. While most electric fretless basses sound quite different than a string bass, the unique quality of a fretless instrument makes it a valuable tool in the bass player's toolbox. Like five- and six-string basses, these instruments are not recommended for beginning players.

Amplifiers and Processors

While the world of bass technology is much more straightforward than that of keyboards or guitars, bass players do rely on some important tools to achieve a great sound. In the following paragraphs, we'll discover how these tools are best used in a worship setting.

Bass amplifiers in worship

Because electric basses rely upon amplification to be heard, bassists are challenged to find a great-sounding solution that is also appropriate for a worship environment. Large amplifiers with large speakers may indeed provide the player with a great deal of *bottom-end* while playing; but in worship, it might become a distraction to the congregation or overwhelm the rest of the instruments. Like guitar amps, bass amps are configured as separate components (amplifier and speakers) or as *combos* (amplifier and speakers combined in one unit). There is no real sonic advantage to one or the other. There are excellent solutions in either configuration. A combo amp can be easier to move around since it's all in one piece, whereas separate components offer the benefit of being able to upgrade or swap out the amp or speakers individually.

In choosing a bass amp, it's important to consider the type of music being played as well as the desired volume level. Some bass amps are better suited to rock styles while others are more

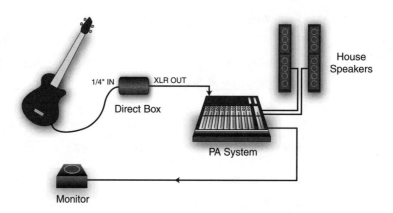

1/4" IN
XLR OUT
Direct Box
PA System
House Speakers
Monitor

versatile and offer the player a more pristine sound suitable for other styles. Many bass players choose to go without an amplifier, instead plugging their bass directly into the main sound system. Depending on the quality of the sound system, this can be a great solution. To do this, the bass signal needs to be inserted into a *direct box*, which then feeds the mixing board input with a standard microphone cable. It's vitally important in this situation to provide bass players with a good monitoring situation so that they can hear themselves play. Because the electric bass guitar makes no sound on its own, bassists cannot hear what they are playing any other way.

Recently, *modeling amplifiers* have made their way into the hands of bass players as well as guitar players. These amplifiers recreate the sounds of the world's best-known amplifiers, putting thousands of dollars worth of performance in the hands of the bassist for a fraction of the cost! Many of these modeling amps also contain common bass effects.

Max Murphy is a worship leader who frequently leads from the electric bass. He teaches and leads worship at Lutheran High School in Orange, California, as well as his home church, St. John's Lutheran, also in Orange, California. Max believes that in a worship context the sound of the bass should come primarily from the main sound system, and not from the bass player's amp. Therefore, he encourages young bass players to plug directly into a *direct box*, which feeds both the main sound system *and* a small combo amp. Max also points out that many congregations are beginning to use *in-ear monitoring* systems. In this context, a bass amp may not be necessary at all.

Bass processors in worship

Bass sounds tend to be more straightforward than guitar sounds. But that doesn't mean that bass players don't have creative options to shape their sounds. While most tone shaping takes place in the amplifier and the bass itself, it's still common to find a few effects in an experienced bass player's rig. Many of these effects are special effects and rarely used in worship. The most commonly used bass effects in worship are *chorus*, *compression*, and *EQ*.

Chorus, as you may remember from Chapter Six, is an effect where the original signal is mixed with a slightly detuned signal to create a thickening of the sound.

Compression, also detailed in Chapter Six, is a dynamics tool that regulates the player's dynamics by making soft passages louder and loud passages softer. This provides a smoother sound and more sustain.

EQ or Equalization is essentially a specialized version of the bass and treble knobs on your car stereo. While any good bass amplifier will have all the EQ you'll ever need, an EQ pedal or effect can help compensate for a weakness in the instrument, amplifier, or P.A. system by boosting or reducing certain frequencies in the sound.

Similar to guitar technology, there are *multi-effect processors* available for bass players. These devices often do more than create effects for the bass. Some of the devices also provide amplifier and speaker modeling as well. Like their guitar counterparts, some of the advanced-modeling processors require a special bass pickup.

The V-Bass from Roland contains both amplifier models and common bass effects. It's compatible with any standard bass guitar equipped with the Roland GK-2B pickup.

Playing Bass in a Worship Context

When we discussed the role of the keyboard player, we touched on the bass player's role as well. In Chapter Five, we defined that role as *to anchor the harmony by emphasizing root movement in a rhythmic partnership with the drums.* That rather academic-sounding definition can be boiled down to two things:

- *The bass player needs to define the chord changes.* While this is not solely the bass player's responsibility, the bass player has the unique role of *anchoring* the music. Because of the harmonic range of the bass, no other instrument can provide that sense of sure footing for the other instruments. It's very much like the foundation of a house. Fancy windows and woodwork don't mean much if the foundation is not well built. A good bass player provides a rock-solid foundation for the music.

- *The bass player needs to partner with the drummer.* Many people mistakenly view the drummer as the timekeeper of the band. The truth is, *all* the instruments share in this responsibility. Nevertheless, no two instruments are as inseparable as bass and drums. The way this works in reality is that the bassist plays the same rhythms that the drummer plays on the kick drum. But this is not a *copycat* arrangement. Rather it's a give-and-take relationship. The drummer is listening to the bass player as much as the bass player is listening to the drummer. The key here is that the two form a rhythmic partnership that helps dictate the *feel*, or *groove*, of the song.

***

The bass player has a great deal of responsibility in a worship setting. He must lay the foundation for the harmony of the song. He's also part of a rhythmic partnership that reinforces the feel and guards the tempo. Bass technology plays an important, but somewhat transparent, role in a bass player's success. In other words, adding a great deal of effects to a bass sound is most likely counterproductive, as it will begin to undermine the bassist's role in the ensemble. So the key thing for bass players to remember, is to embrace their role and make sure that any effects are supportive in nature to the worship environment.

EIGHT

ELECTRONIC PERCUSSION IN WORSHIP

Not since the debut of the pipe organ have we seen an instrument that has caused more controversy in worship music. While much of the controversy can be attributed to a style bias, the acoustic design of traditional houses of worship has not helped the matter. While a room with *live* acoustics enhances the sound of a choir or a pipe organ, it can make acoustic drums difficult to use—even for their most passionate advocates. The advent of great sounding, affordable, and easy-to-use electronic musical instruments brought with it a great deal of promise for drummers in the church. Today's electronic percussion instruments have delivered on that promise in a big way. In this chapter, we'll explore the world of electronic percussion, focusing our attention on practical solutions that will begin to erase the stigma that has surrounded drummers and percussionists in the church. Here's what we'll cover:

- Types of electronic percussion instruments
- Key advantages of using electronic percussion in worship
- Tips for successful use of electronic percussion in worship

The goal of this chapter is to demystify the world of electronic percussion, enabling these powerful instruments to overcome any lingering controversy, and show their value as ministry tools that enhance the worship experience.

Types of Electronic Percussion Instruments

Electronic percussion instruments first became widely available in the 1970s and 1980s. However, because of their high price and synthetic sound, it wasn't until the mid-1990s that electronic percussion began to appear in houses of worship on any kind of scale. While those early instruments were mostly *drum sets*, today's instruments include compelling options for both drummers and hand percussionists.

The electronic drum kit

An electronic drum kit includes several *drum pads* that take the place of each drum and cymbal in a common acoustic drum kit. This would normally include a kick drum, snare drum, at least a couple of tom-toms, a high-hat cymbal, and at least two additional cymbals. Each *pad* is positioned the way it would be in a common drum kit. Each pad is played in the same way that an acoustic drum kit is played. The kick drum pad is played with a standard kick drum pedal. The other pads are struck with conventional drumsticks. This is part of the appeal of electronic drums. The difference is found in how the pads generate sound.

The playing surface on electronic drum pads is usually made of a rubberized material or a nylon mesh. These pads are designed to make very little sound when struck. To create sound, they are connected to a special drum sound module via standard instrument cables. Each drum pad is velocity sensitive and, when struck, sends a signal to the sound module, triggering a sampled percussion instrument. The sound module contains a variety of different *drum kit* configurations. Like *patches* on a synthesizer, drum kits can be changed at the touch of a single button. This makes it easy to choose a kit that best suits the music being played. Drum kits can also be customized to include any combination of instruments. If a song requires both classical and contemporary sounds, a few of the pads can be assigned to timpani and the rest to regular acoustic drum set sounds.

Like synthesizers, a conventional electronic drum kit uses digitally recorded samples to create sound. When a drummer strikes the snare pad on an electronic drum kit, the signal sent from the pad *triggers* a real snare drum sample from the sound module. Each sound can be played with the same level of expression that keyboard players enjoy. If the pad is hit very hard, the sound will be loud. If the pad is hit softly, the sound will be soft. Like keyboards, many electronic drum kits also use *velocity switching* to create a more musical performance. Different sounds can be triggered from the same pad, depending on how hard the pad is hit. This is especially helpful with cymbals, as it provides more color to the overall sound. Electronic drum kits also enjoy powerful MIDI capabilities. This allows future expansion of sounds as well as MIDI performance and sequencing capabilities that were previously available only to keyboard players.

The Roland V-Drums utilize modeling technology to create a wide variety of percussion sounds. The pads are designed to be played with sticks or brushes, and the mesh drumhead provides a realistic feel for the drummer. The V-Drums' positional-sensing capability allows the drummer to change the character of each drum and cymbal depending on where the stick strikes the pad. The Roland TD-20 percussion sound module includes over 750 sounds, including 50 full drum kits. It also has onboard effects, such as reverb, EQ, and compression.

Drum-modeling instruments

Recently, a few instruments have surfaced that utilize acoustic-modeling technology to faithfully emulate percussive instruments. Although slightly more expensive than traditional sample-based electronic drum kits, these kits have brought a new level of realism to electronic percussion. Modeled percussion instruments also use ultra-realistic drum and cymbal pads. These pads are far more natural-feeling—comparable to what a drummer is used to playing. As a result, they provide a greater amount of expression to the music. Drum-modeling instruments are designed to capture every nuance of a drummer's performance and translate that performance into an authentic emulation of acoustic percussion instruments. Modeling drum kits are capable of *positional sensing*. This emulates the acoustic drummer's ability to alter the sound based on *where* the drum or cymbal, is struck. These tools are so powerful that many drummers choose to use modeling drum kits even when an acoustic kit is an option!

Other electronic percussion instruments

In recent years, a number of other electronic percussion instruments have become commonplace in houses of worship. Although there is some variety among these devices, this group can be broken down as follows:

- Compact electronic percussion instruments
- Electronic hand percussion instruments

The Roland SPD-20 Compact Percussion Pad with optional kick, hi-hat and snare triggers

Compact electronic percussion instruments grew out of the need for an electronic percussion solution that was extremely space and budget conscious. What if you want a full array of drum and percussion sounds, but a full drum kit isn't feasible due to space or budget limitations? These *percussion pad* instruments often take on the appearance of a flat, rectangular drum pad that is divided into six or eight smaller regions—each of which can trigger a different instrument. The percussion sounds are usually built into the pad, but additional sounds can be triggered via MIDI. This makes it possible for percussionists to trigger sounds in a keyboard or sound module from a

percussion pad controller. On some electronic percussion pads you can even plug in pedals to trigger the kick drum and hi-hat sounds. This compact setup can provide a great solution for churches that have either a small space or a small budget! Another common use of these percussion pads is to incorporate them into an acoustic drum kit. This "best of both worlds" solution gives the drummer access to virtually any sound. Latin percussion, timpani, even vocal riffs can be triggered from the percussion pad while keeping the groove on the acoustic kit.

Electronic hand percussion instruments are a relatively new instrument group. Upon seeing the incredible palette of sounds available to drummers, musicians who specialize in hand percussion instruments began to dream of their own electronic instrument. That dream has become a reality with the introduction of the Handsonic by Roland. This incredibly powerful instrument allows access to 600 instruments from Latin countries, Asia, India, and more. It

The Roland HPD-15 Handsonic

utilizes *positional sensing* on its 10" rubber surface, which has fifteen separate pads—each of which can trigger a separate sound simultaneously. The Handsonic has a built-in sequencer as well as full MIDI implementation.

Advantages of Electronic Percussion

Although the benefits are many, the single most celebrated advantage of electronic percussion in a worship setting is *volume control*. Because the drum pads on an electronic kit make very little sound, virtually all of the music comes from the main sound system. This gives the person at the mixing board complete control of the drum volume in the room. Because the worship space is not always advantageous acoustically, and because drummers are not always adept at playing with sensitivity, electronic percussion offers a practical solution that can overcome both the room and the drummer who won't "turn down."

Another key advantage of electronic percussion instruments is the variety of sounds that are available in a worship setting. While an experienced drummer can coax a great deal of tonal variety out of a common drum kit, there's no escaping the fact that it's still "a drum kit." Electronic percussion allows us to experience orchestral, Latin, Asian, or Indian percussion instruments as well as a traditional drum kit all *with the push of a single button*!

Yet another key advantage of electronic percussion in worship is portability. For those churches that meet in a rented space, setting up and tearing down each week can be quite draining. Any solution that limits storage space or setup time is invaluable. For churches that don't have much physical space for their musicians, electronic percussion instruments can be a great solution. And for those worship settings that regularly change venues (small groups, rehearsals, home studies, etc.), electronic percussion instruments can provide a quick and easy solution.

Although he can regularly be found in the studio recording a jingle or in the orchestra pit for shows like the Los Angeles production of *The Lion King*, David Owens feels most at home while playing drums and percussion in a worship setting. He participates in the worship at Plymouth Church in Whittier, California, his home church, and is a frequent guest at a variety of other Southern California churches. Like most percussionists, David grew up playing acoustic instruments. But his background hasn't kept him from embracing electronic instruments. David not only plays electronic percussion, he's often called upon to teach workshops on the subject.

When asked what advice he would offer those who are new to electronic percussion, he responded firmly, "Homework is involved!" David believes that one of the most common mistakes that church drummers make is to assume that they can just sit down and play. "We don't expect that from a new computer. Why then do we expect that from an electronic instrument?" he adds. David points out that every drummer has their own style when playing an acoustic drum kit. He believes that today's technology has advanced to the point where electronic instruments can be made to respond to each player's unique style of playing. So he encourages musicians to spend a few *homework* hours getting familiar with the capabilities of an electronic percussion instrument.

Using electronic percussion in worship

You might notice a theme developing here: Understanding your role in a worship ensemble has less to do with what you're doing on your instrument, and more to do with what others are doing. In other words, our role is to *fit* in a way that enhances the music and the unity of the team. The role of the percussionist changes a bit depending on the instrument being played and the style of the song. But what doesn't change is the responsibility to keep good time and to only play what complements the other musician's parts. This is not limited to the notes or rhythms that we play but also to the sounds we choose. In worship, we need to think of the *song lyrics*, *the congregation*, and the *worship team* when we choose both our sounds and musical parts. Electronic percussionists have hundreds of sounds at their disposal. But just because we *can* doesn't mean we *should*. In a traditional congregation that's just getting started with drums, it's best to start with a softer-sounding kit. A huge-sounding rock drum kit would likely be an insensitive choice. Likewise, a very synthetic-sounding kit might be out of step with an ensemble that's made up of very acoustic-sounding instruments. The key here is to practice deference in our playing and in our sound choices. Take baby steps. A small success serves your larger vision. This is never more true than when introducing instruments, electronic or otherwise, to your ministry.

In addition to serving your musical vision, electronic percussion can also serve as a ministry-building tool. As we discussed in Chapter Six with guitar technology, there are many ways that electronic percussion can be used to include others into your ministry. As with guitarists, there are probably some drummers hiding in your pews. They don't have to be professionals to make a meaningful contribution, and electronic drums offer many opportunities. Besides, the great thing about them is that they can always be turned down!

- Electronic percussion provides a great opportunity to include less-experienced players who might not be ready to serve as the primary percussionist in the worship service, but could contribute by adding supplemental percussion parts.

- Even assigning a player to a single pad on a kit goes a long way toward inclusiveness in worship, as well as providing a stepping-stone for a young player who is seeking to grow. In the meantime, they're getting the experience of playing with better musicians and growing spiritually under your guidance.

Electronic percussion can also add new dimensions to an acoustic drum kit

NINE

HARD DISK
RECORDING IN A
WORSHIP SETTING

Hard disk recording is the ability to record sound to a hard disk. In Chapter Four, we briefly touched on the concept of hard disk recording as it relates to MIDI sequencing. But unlike sequencing, which records only MIDI instructions, hard disk recording allows the user to create CD quality (or better) audio recordings of vocals or any acoustic instrument. In this chapter, we'll learn how hard disk recording works, as well as how it can be used to enrich your church's worship ministry.

A Brief History of Hard Disk Recording

Beginning in 1979 with the introduction of the *Fairlight CMI (Computer Musical Instrument)*, the race was on to put digital recording capabilities into the hands of musicians. While these early devices were instruments that played digitally recorded *samples*, manufacturers could predict a day when *entire songs* could be recorded using digital technology. Throughout the 1980s and early 1990s, a variety of companies devel-

Fairlight CMI

oped technology that could record audio to a computer hard disk. But these systems were out of reach for most musicians due to their high prices and complicated operation. In 1996, the Roland Corporation shocked the music world by releasing the VS-880, the world's first stand-alone hard disk recorder that was both affordable and easy to use. This tabletop piece of hardware included extensive editing capabilities as well as digital effects and could play back as many as eight tracks of CD-quality audio. Musicians were able to create great-sounding digital recordings of their music and even burn their own CDs without the need for high-priced recording studios.

Software-based hard disk recording solutions followed a similar path in the 1990s. These products were simply software applications that allowed the musician to use a personal computer as a hard disk recorder. However, unlike the VS-880, software-based hard disk recorders required expensive computers as well as additional hardware in order to convert the sound into a digital signal.

Today, hard disk recording is accessible to virtually all musicians. The musical journey in which a song travels from an idea to a finished compact disc has been shortened considerably. Affordable, easy-to-use hard disk recorders are readily available in either hardware or software versions. Let's look at how hard disk recording works.

How does it work?

The main concept that needs to be grasped is the difference between *analog* and *digital* audio. Although we may not know it, many of us are familiar with analog recording. In fact, until recently all recordings were analog recordings. In analog recording, sound is recorded as an electrical signal onto a thin strip of plastic that is coated with magnetic particles. Making a recording onto a cassette tape is an example of analog recording. Digital recording differs from analog recording in that sound is *converted* to a digital format during the recording process. This is accomplished with an *analog-to-digital converter (ADC)*, which turns the sound into a language that a computer can understand. This language is a stream of numbers called *binary code*. Binary code consists of 1s and 0s (bits) that can be stored on a hard disk. This information is retrieved from the hard disk and translated by a *digital-to-analog converter (DAC)* in order to play back the music.

So, what makes a great digital recorder? There is a considerable amount of diversity among experts as to what elements contribute most to creating high quality digital sound. For our purposes here, we won't seek to cover any new ground on this issue. Rather, we'll identify and define some key concepts and terms that relate to hard disk recording technology.

Sampling rate

Hard disk recording is accomplished when a computer takes a series of *pictures* of the sound. These pictures are called *samples* and are recorded over time. The number of samples that are recorded in one second is called the *sampling rate* (see diagram on pg. 114). Although there are other variables involved, we can assume that the higher the sampling rate, the higher quality the sound will be. The standard sampling rate for CD-quality sound is 44.1kHz, or 44,100 *samples per second*. Many hard disk recorders now offer sampling rates that are over twice that rate.

How sampling rate affects sound quality:

If a sound wave looks like this
over the course of one second...

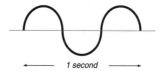

...and we take four samples
of it at equal time
intervals...

...the resulting digitized sound wave might
look like this, since it reflects what the wave
was doing as each sample was captured.

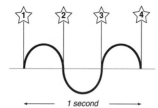 =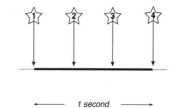

The more samples we capture, the more accurate a
representation we get of the original sound wave.

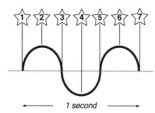 =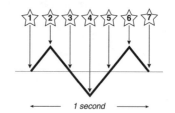

Bit depth

While the sampling rate is a very important element in digital recording quality, the

A 16-bit word	A 24-bit word
00110101 11101000	11001010 10100011 00111000

resolution of each sample is equally important. The resolution, or *bit depth*, represents the *dynamic range* of a sample. The dynamic range refers to the number of volume levels a sample is capable of reproducing. We've already established that a digital recording consists of 1s and 0s (bits) called *binary code*. A 1-bit sample is only capable of reproducing two levels of volume—off or on (0 or 1). The standard for CD-quality audio is 16-bit, which provides for 65,536 levels of dynamic range—obviously, much more realistic. Many hard disk recorders allow the user to record at 24-bit resolution. Again, there are other factors involved, but the general concept is that greater bit depth equals higher-quality audio.

Recording and playback

Although digital and analog recording technologies are quite different, most digital recorders have familiar analog-style con-

Transport buttons

trols in order to simplify use. The *record, play,* and *stop* buttons do just what we'd expect them to. But *how* they work is another story. Digital recording is sometimes called *non-linear recording.* This is because it doesn't conform to the constraints of analog recording. In analog recording, the recording process is sequential or *linear* in nature. The beginning of the song is recorded at the beginning of the tape. The end of the song would be found several feet of tape later. Digital recording, on the other hand, is non-sequential. There's no beginning or end to the hard disk upon which digital audio is recorded. It's completely *non-linear.* This provides a significant advantage. While it takes time to *cue up* (locate) the beginning of a song on analog tape, finding the beginning of a song on a hard disk recorder occurs instantaneously at the click of a mouse or at the touch of a single button! We can even mark key places within our music for quick access. These places are called *markers,* or *locators,* and they, too, can be accessed instantaneously—no waiting while searching around with *fast-forward* and *rewind.* A major New York studio once did a study to determine how much time was wasted in a year, waiting for tape to rewind. The answer: six weeks!

Editing

Hard disk recording is similar to MIDI sequencing in that extensive *editing* capabilities are available. Because we are

Non-linear editing

essentially dealing with information (the binary code), hard disk recorders provide the ability to *edit* the music after it's been recorded. Virtually all hard disk recorders allow the user to *mix,* or adjust, the volume levels of the various recorded tracks. Many hardware and software hard disk recording solutions provide the ability to add various types of digital effects to the recorded tracks as well. But perhaps the most exciting capability is found in the hard disk recorder's ability to *cut, copy,* and *paste* audio! Like MIDI sequencing, hard disk recorders provide the ability to move audio forward or backward. We can copy a part we like and move it to another part of the song. We can even piece together several different *takes,* or versions, of a track to create a more compelling performance. The key here is flexibility. Never before has this kind of capability been in the hands of worship leaders!

Latency

During hard disk recording, an acoustic sound source such as a microphone signal travels through the *analog-to-digital converter*, is stored to disk, then travels through the *digital-to-analog converter* in order to be heard during playback.

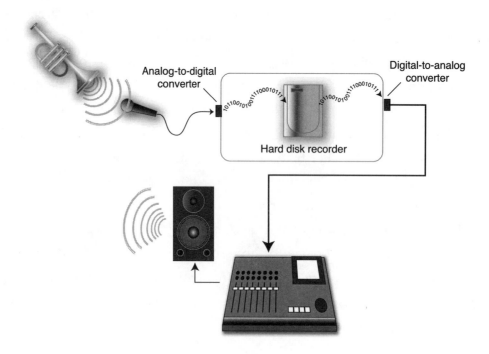

Although this journey happens very quickly, there is a certain amount of delay between the moment the sound first reaches the hard disk recorder's inputs and the moment the sound leaves the recorder's outputs. This delay is called *latency*. All hard disk recorders introduce some level of latency to the process. That's not the issue. Rather, the issue is found in *how much* latency is introduced. Latency becomes an issue when the delay is so great that it introduces an unwanted echo effect during recording. The vocalist sings a note and hears it back a half second after it was sung. This is not a desirable effect and can be quite distracting! The good news is that latency can be reduced to a level that is inaudible. Stand-alone hard disk recorders are built in such a way that there is virtually zero latency. This is one of the big advantages of these systems. In computer- or software-based systems, however, excessive latency is more prevalent. It can be caused by software that isn't optimally configured, a slow computer processor, too little RAM, or a slow audio interface. Be sure to read the documentation that comes with your software and audio interface in order to optimize your settings.

Software-based Hard Disk Recording

Setting up a software-based hard disk recording system is not unlike setting up a MIDI sequencing system. In fact, most hard disk recording software includes both MIDI sequencing and hard disk recording capability. Here's what you'll need:

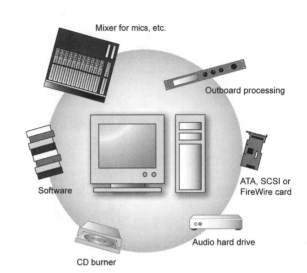

Mixer for mics, etc.

Outboard processing

ATA, SCSI or FireWire card

Software

Audio hard drive

CD burner

- *Hard disk recording software:* There are quite a few software titles to choose from at prices from $100 to $1,000. Differences between programs have to do with the number of tracks available, whether or not MIDI sequencing is included, editing capabilities, the type of compatible digital effects, the graphic layout, and so on.

- *Audio interface:* This is the device that serves as the *analog-to-digital (A/D)* and *digital-to-analog (D/A) converter.* Although many computers have audio inputs, they're typically limited to a stereo signal and the audio quality is not very good. An external audio interface connects to your computer via USB, FireWire, or a PCI card slot. Many audio interfaces provide multiple inputs and outputs. Some even allow a microphone to be connected directly.

- *Computer:* While the platform (Mac or PC) is not so important anymore, there are a couple of things to remember to ensure a pleasant recording experience. First, audio recording requires a great deal of RAM (memory). It's a good rule of thumb to purchase as much RAM as you can afford (or your machine can accommodate). Second, unlike MIDI sequencing, hard disk recording puts quite a drain on your computer processor. So, you'll want to use the fastest computer possible. Finally, audio files take up a great deal of hard disk space. Therefore, it's wise to plan for additional hard disk space in advance. It's common to use more than one hard drive when doing hard disk recording on a computer. It's also a good idea to use a high-performance hard drive. Most experts recommend that a hard drive be at least 7,200 RPM in order to accommodate digital audio. There are many affordable hard drives that meet this specification.

- *MIDI interface:* If your hard disk recording system will also involve MIDI sequencing, then you'll need a MIDI interface. Some audio interfaces also have MIDI ports so you can get away with one piece of hardware doing double duty.

The Edirol UA-1000 USB 2.0 Audio/MIDI Interface

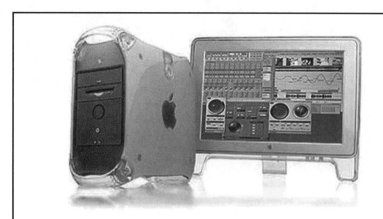

Digital Performer, from Mark of the Unicorn, integrates digital audio recording and MIDI-sequencing capabilities and is a popular choice among worship leaders who use a Macintosh computer.

The example at right shows a typical configuration for a software-based hard disk recording system. In this example, the analog signal from the microphone is converted to a digital signal at the audio interface and sent to the computer via a FireWire cable. Once the audio is recorded to the computer's hard disk, the sound can be manipulated using a variety of *plug-in* (software based) effects like reverb, delay, chorus, etc.

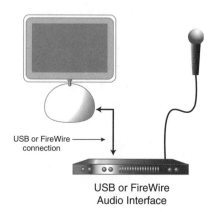

USB or FireWire connection

USB or FireWire Audio Interface

Although recording and editing capabilities differ between software programs, there are some common features of hard disk recording software:

- *MIDI integration:* Hard disk recording software is a great option for those who already use their computers for MIDI sequencing. In fact, it's likely that your MIDI sequencing software already has, or can be, upgraded to have digital audio recording capability.

- *Graphically friendly:* Hard disk recording software provides an easy-to-navigate, color-coded interface for those who have large computer monitors. Some musicians even use dual-monitor systems for hard disk recording.

- *Easily upgradeable:* Hard disk recording software is regularly updated by the manufacturer.

- *Plug-ins:* Hard disk recording software usually allows third-party software companies to write additional software that can be added to provide various editing and effect capabilities. These additional software applications, called *plug-ins*, are written to conform to a standard file format to ensure compatibility with a wide variety of hard disk recording software. VST, DXi, TDM, RTAS, MAS, and AU are examples of these standards. To find out which plug-in formats are supported by your software, check the documentation.

- *CD burning:* Once you've finished recording and mixing a song, most hard disk recording software can export the song to a .WAV or AIFF file for CD burning. Since most computers are equipped with CD-burning capabilities, this is a relatively seamless process.

- *Portability:* With the introduction of FireWire and USB audio interfaces, hard disk recording software can now be used with laptop computers. This provides a great deal of flexibility in choosing the recording environment.

Stand-alone Hard Disk Recorders

Beginning with the introduction of the Roland VS-880 in 1996, there has been a steady stream of innovation in stand-alone hard disk recorders. While the VS-880 had some rather modest limitations, today's products are every bit as powerful as their software-based counterparts. Here are some advantages to stand-alone hard disk recorders:

The original Roland VS-880 Digital Studio Workstation

- *Integration:* Perhaps the greatest advantage to stand-alone hard disk recorders is integration. These *digital studio workstations* contain all the necessary hardware and software in one device, including an audio interface, a digital mixing console, editing capability, and digital effects. Many units have built-in CD burners as well. The key advantage here is that it's a complete turnkey solution. There is no configuration required. There are no compatibility issues. It's truly plug-and-play.

- *Portability:* Another key advantage of stand-alone units is portability. Most digital studio workstations are tabletop units that are easily moved. Unlike laptop computer systems, stand-alone recorders are completely self-contained. The audio interface, software, effects, and mixing board are all *housed under one roof*! Only one power switch, only one thing to plug in.

- *Near-zero latency:* Because of the tight integration between components in a stand-alone digital studio, latency is virtually inaudible and not a factor during recording.

The VS series lives! Roland has continued the heritage of the original VS-880 with their flagship VS-2480DVD. The VS-2480DVD can play back up to 24 tracks, includes a 64-channel digital mixer with 17 motorized faders, expandable effects with 3rd party plugin compatibility and a built-in DVD burner. It even has a VGA monitor output for those who want a large, color graphic display (display optional).

Using Hard Disk Recording in a Worship Context

At first glance, the benefits of hard disk recording may not be readily apparent to some worship leaders. After all, as musicians, we're about the business of creating *live* worship music. But if we stop there, we'll miss some good stuff. Here are some practical applications for hard disk recording that can enrich your worship ministry:

- *Background tracks:* In Chapter Four, we learned about creating sequences to supplement, or even replace an ensemble if needed. Hard disk recording adds to that capability by giving us the ability to record backing vocals, guitars, percussion, or any other acoustic instrument. The rules are still the same—don't forget a click track for reference!

- *Rehearsal tracks:* Learning vocal parts was never so easy (and fun). Provide your vocalists with a great way to practice their parts while at home or in the car. Create a simple instrumental track and record each vocal part to a separate track. You can easily make multiple versions of each song so that each harmony part can be heard by itself, then as part of the group. You'll find that rehearsal will become much more efficient if your vocalists are showing up with their parts already learned!

If you want to get really efficient, you can send audio to your team via the Internet. The audio tracks that you burn to a CD can just as easily be converted into an mp3 file using a program like iTunes. This significantly reduces the size of the CD audio file, which is a massive 10 MB per minute of audio. Upload the mp3 to a special section of the church website that only the team knows about, or you can simply email the mp3 files to team members.

Stephen Claybrook, worship pastor at Crosspointe Church in Cary, North Carolina, uses hard disk recording to create supplemental backing tracks for worship. Like many worship leaders, Stephen finds that he doesn't always have enough musicians to even come close to the instrumentation that he hears on many contemporary Christian songs. But rather than pass on a great song, Stephen creates a recording that includes whatever musicians he's missing in order to effectively communicate the song. This might include vocals, guitar, percussion, keyboard, or any number of other parts.

Stephen creates the recording on his Macintosh using MOTU's Digital Performer. After creating the final mix, he burns a CD, which is used for playback in the service. Stephen finds that if his recording includes percussion parts, a click track may not be necessary as a tempo reference for the band. If necessary, he creates a CD with a click track that is panned to the far left of the stereo spectrum while the music is panned to the far right. This allows the sound engineer to split the signal. Only the right channel (the music track) goes to the main sound system and is heard by the congregation. The left channel (click track) of the CD would be fed to the drummer's headphones as a tempo reference.

- *Songwriting:* Many congregations are using songs for worship that were written by staff or members of the congregation. Hard disk recording is a great tool for transforming an ambiguous idea in someone's head to a very tangible (and great sounding) song.

- *Worship recordings:* An increasing number of churches are discovering that recording and releasing a worship CD can enhance the worship life of their congregation. Using hard disk recording to create a worship CD gives people an opportunity to take home the music they sing in the worship service. By recording the CD using your own hard disk recording system, it pays for itself.

- *Service CDs:* There are numerous benefits to recording your services. Many churches are investing in a CD duplicator and making CDs available in the church bookstore following the service. This is a great way for parishioners to take the music and the message with them into the world. They share it with friends, co-workers, family, etc. It's also a great way to bring your ministry to shut-ins and the infirmed who can't get to church.

  If your church has a website, you can easily convert the digital audio from the CD into an mp3 file and make it available from the Internet.

  Plus, in the same way that a coach reviews game films with the players following a game, a CD of the service is an excellent training tool. There's nothing more affirming (and convincing) than a recording—the CD doesn't lie! Discuss what worked and why, and what didn't work and how to fix it.

- *Recording rehearsals:* In the same way that listening to recordings of your services can bring an objective perspective to the table, recording rehearsals with a portable studio can provide immediate feedback. If a spontaneous song breaks out and it sounds great, you've captured it. Also, if something worked great in rehearsal on Thursday night, and now, for some reason, on Sunday morning at sound check it's not happening, play back the recording.

- *Kid's music:* It's not just the adult ministries that can benefit from a portable digital studio. Set up a couple of microphones, record the kid's choir concert and then burn a CD. Have the kids help design some art for the packaging. Send it out for duplication or have the kids do it in-house. This is a fun and educational project that will pay for a digital recorder the first time you do it. Every parent, aunt, grandmother, and godparent will buy one for $5. It probably costs about $1.50 to produce. The kids have just helped to pay their way to camp.

Tips for Using Hard Disk Recording in Worship

Like other music technologies, hard disk recording can be a powerful enhancement to worship if used properly. The key is keeping the technology *transparent* in worship. In other words, if hard disk recording is used in such a way that it becomes the center of attention, it will undoubtedly distract the congregation from their focus. So how do we ensure that hard disk recording is a blessing? Consider the following tips:

- *Use hard disk recording to enhance existing instrument or vocal parts.* In other words, create an additional guitar part to add to your live guitar part. This will create a thicker, warmer, fuller sound. If you have a handful of string players, consider having them record their parts ahead of time (maybe even twice to thicken it up). Then, during the worship service, they'll be playing with a string section that sounds two or three times as rich as it would if they were on their own.

- *Use hard disk recording to add missing instrument or vocal parts.* This is a trickier endeavor, as it's easy to go overboard and lose that technological *transparency* that we need to shoot for. But the fact remains that most of us don't have 80-piece orchestras in our congregations. But tools like MIDI sequencers and hard disk recorders provide us with incredible capabilities to put instruments or vocals where we formerly didn't have them! The key here is to keep the recording supplemental in nature. Try to put *live people* in the most prominent musical roles. This might take some *trial* and hopefully not too much *error*, but it's well worth the effort.

- *Use hard disk recording to mentor younger players.* Create *music-minus-one* tracks for your less-experienced instrumentalists. This is simply a recording of a song with a particular instrument removed. A guitar player, for example, can play along with the recording with the guitar part removed and hear himself play along. This is a great practice tool.

- *Use hard disk recording to create rehearsal tracks for vocalists.* Like creating tracks for instrumentalists, this can be an extremely powerful tool for building up your vocal team. Rehearsal CDs allow vocalists to grow outside of rehearsal, allowing them to practice on their own time. You'll find that this will result in an exponential improvement in your vocalists' confidence and preparation!

- *Use hard disk recording to develop and empower your lay leaders.* Hard disk recording offers a way for you to leverage your time by delegating leadership in rehearsals. While you're working with the instrumentalists, send a vocal team leader off with the rest of the vocalists. He or she may not have keyboard skills, but his or her leadership and musicianship can still be utilized with a stand-alone hard disk recorder. Put the vocal parts and the keyboard or instrumental part on individual tracks. Set up marker points for the verse, chorus, etc. The leader can easily isolate each track for teaching parts, and jump around to different sections of the song quickly.

- *Use a hard disk recorder as a digital accompanist.* If you rely on an accompanist for rehearsals, it pays to have that person come in for a few hours and record the accompaniments for a dozen songs you'll be doing in the next few months. Now you have an accompaniment track upon which you can record the vocal parts for making rehearsal CDs and to use in sectionals. Plus, you're covered in case your accompanist calls in sick.

- *Use hard disk recording to introduce new music to your congregation.* If your church has songwriters that write new worship material, consider distributing recordings of that material to the congregation *before* you introduce it in a worship service. Consider it a *rehearsal recording* of sorts for your congregation. This way, they can become familiar with the song before its debut. *Of course, if you're using published material, you'll need to comply with copyright law.*

The BOSS BR-1600 is an inexpensive, portable recording studio

TEN

MUSIC TECHNOLOGY IN A SMALL CHURCH SETTING

At this point in our journey through the world of music technology, it's possible that you might be thinking, "This is all wonderful and I can definitely see the possibilities, but my vision is bigger than my budget." According to various statistical sources, the average congregation in America is less than a hundred people. Given those numbers, finding musicians in even an average-sized church is difficult. What about smaller churches? What about new churches? Are smaller churches with smaller resources out in the cold when it comes to using music technology? *Absolutely not!* In this chapter, we'll explore some very practical ways in which small churches with small budgets can use electronic music technology.

MIDI Sequencing

As we learned in Chapter Four, MIDI sequencing can be a powerful addition to any ministry. Because MIDI sequencing essentially gives a church extra musicians, the benefits to small churches may be greatest. While sequencing can make a good band sound better, in a small church it can enable one or two musicians to sound like ten, twenty, or even more!

Start slowly! When adding any new technology, it's best to use it sparingly at first. In order to integrate MIDI sequencing into your worship service, choose one or two popular hymns or choruses to start with. Then, add another every couple weeks. This keeps the expectations realistic and keeps your workload manageable.

If you're a worship leader who leads from the guitar without any other instruments, consider sequencing a pad or string part along with a light percussion part like a *shaker* or *congas* (or both). If you're a keyboard player, add a bass part and a percussion part. You don't have to emulate a full rhythm section. You may find that sequencing one or two parts maintains the intimacy of your group, while a lot of tracks can put the technology front and center, detracting from the worship.

Powerful keyboard *workstations* can be purchased for around $2,000. This is a complete solution. However, if you already have a computer, basic-sequencing software can be purchased for less than $100. Multitimbral keyboards start under $1,000. Sound modules can be had for about half of that. As you can see, these powerful ministry tools are well within the reach of most small churches.

General MIDI Files

Many small churches use commercially available General MIDI files as accompaniment tracks for worship. In Chapter Four, we learned that General MIDI files adhere to an industry-wide standard in order to be compatible with any General MIDI playback device. Because of the flexibility of these MIDI files, they're a very popular option for churches that have few or no instrumentalists. Remember, with General MIDI files, the tempo or pitch can be easily changed. Instruments can be changed or muted as well. This allows a congregation to gradually add instrumentalists as they become available. Commercial MIDI files are generally available in bundles, which are an economical way of building a library.

Hard Disk Recording

Hard disk recording can be used in a small church situation in much the same way that MIDI sequencing is. Stand-alone *digital-studio workstations* are especially good as they are inexpensive and very portable. Songs can be played right from the hard disk recorder, bypassing the need to burn a CD. Small churches can benefit from extra guitar parts, bass parts, string parts, even vocal parts. Remember, the key is to start slowly, always mindful of keeping the technology in a supportive role. Stand-alone digital studios start well under $1,000 and often include a mixing console and digital effects.

Choosing a Keyboard in a Small Church Setting

Small churches are often dependent on hiring a keyboardist to accompany their services. While some keyboard players prefer to supply their own keyboard, many churches find themselves in need of acquiring a keyboard for worship. Here are a few things to consider before making a decision:

- *How portable does the keyboard need to be?* Many new churches meet in rented or borrowed space and must bring everything they need with them each week. In this case, the size and weight of the instrument are an issue, along with durability. Sound variety and features need to be balanced with durability and portability in order to make a wise decision.

- *Who's going to play it?* In many cases, a church's keyboard will be played by a number of different people over the coming months and years. Therefore it's wise to choose a keyboard that has a wide appeal. If your church doesn't have an acoustic piano, you might want a keyboard with weighted action and 88 keys, as most keyboard players are used to playing piano. Look for a keyboard that has strong sounds in various instrument families. Look for lots of polyphony (at least 64) and the ability to change sounds easily. Quick access to basic editing features as well as keyboard splits and layers are a plus.

- *Is it expandable?* Most small churches don't have the budget to replace their keyboard every couple of years. One of the greatest ways to protect your church's investment is to choose a keyboard that is expandable. Instead of spending thousands every couple years, a modest investment in an expansion board will provide a whole new library of state-of-the-art sounds.

Portable Churches

New churches are often dependent on using rented space for worship. They must transport everything they need in and out each week. Music technology can make this monumental task manageable. Electronic percussion instruments are easier to move and to store than their acoustic counterparts. Guitar- or bass-modeling processors can take the place of large, cumbersome amplifiers. These alternatives can save your team valuable time and energy during the weekly setup process.

***

Due in part to the emergence of powerful technology, small churches are no longer handcuffed in terms of the kind of music they can offer. A modest investment of resources followed by a willingness to learn can go a long way toward providing a *big sound* for your small church!

ELEVEN

MUSIC TECHNOLOGY IN A TRADITIONAL CHURCH SETTING

Through my coaching ministry, Arts Impact, I've worked with a number of traditional churches. Some of these churches are from denominations and traditions that date back over 300 years. The single most common struggle that these churches face is finding a balance between honoring the *heritage* of the church while embracing *the new*. Churches face the fear of reaching out to dialogue with our ever-changing culture at the expense of undervaluing the *time honored*. Must we choose between the two? *Absolutely not!* I firmly believe that a church's heritage is not a liability in terms of reaching a twenty-first century culture. While this is not a book on ministry philosophy, music technology can play a role in how traditional churches can realize these dual objectives.

To address this issue, many churches choose to present two or more music styles in their services. While this can be a successful model, it's also important to provide a unifying factor between the styles. Music technology can assist in that endeavor. For example, many modern church organs are MIDI-capable. If you have a MIDI capable organ, consider using a *sound module* along with the organ. Add some new textures to your sound through creating MIDI layers. String ensemble patches sound great layered with a pipe organ. This can be a great way to enhance the sounds in a traditional service without really changing any of the music!

Another way to bridge the gap is to add a synthesizer to a traditional service. Even liturgical forms will sound wonderful when played with well-chosen patches on a synthesizer. But don't replace the organ on every element of the service. As is the case with any technology,

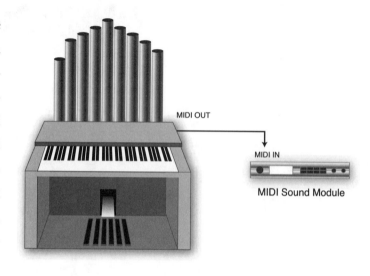

start slowly. Begin with using a synthesizer in a hymn or an element of the liturgy. Choose a patch that isn't a huge departure sonically. Remember, we want to *engage* people, not *distract* them.

If your church has both contemporary and traditional services, consider bringing some traditional elements into the contemporary service (and vice versa). Many churches find that contemporary arrangements of hymns are well received. Some liturgical churches are creating contemporary settings for various elements of the liturgy to integrate into the service. Whatever you choose to do, remember that bridging the gap between the time honored and the new brings a sense of vitality and unity to your worship.

Many traditional churches face resistance when trying to add new instruments to the service. After all, it's human nature to cling to the comfortable and familiar. Adding a keyboard synthesizer to worship may not cause grumblings in your congregation given the synthesizer's ability to create realistic emulation of various traditional instruments. But what about instruments like drums or electric guitar? Is it possible to add electronic instruments like this in a traditional context? I believe it is.

When we get a new car, a new shirt, or a new pet, we're anxious to show it off. We want to share our excitement with everyone we know. The same is true when musicians first discover electronic musical instruments. We want to show off all the sounds that our synthesizers are capable of making. We want to show everyone how an effects processor can change a guitar's sound. While excitement is certainly a good thing, a desire to shove new technology to the front and center of the worship service is a distraction at best and a prelude to conflict at worst.

Several times in this book, we've discussed the importance of music technology remaining *transparent* in the worship service. Never is this more applicable than when introducing new instruments to a congregation. The degree to which our new instruments are noticeable is the degree to which they will become obstacles to engaging the congregation. In coaching congregations through this process, I recommend four things:

- *Change slowly:* If your goal is to add a synthesizer to a traditional service, create a schedule over a reasonable amount of time that spells out how this will happen. Not only will it provide you with a road map, but it will also help you to manage your expectations. For example, if your goal is to split the music evenly between organ and synthesizer, consider playing one hymn per week on the synthesizer for six weeks. During the next six weeks, play the prelude on the synthesizer each week. Continue this schedule until you've reached your goal.

- *Change subtly:* If you're planning on adding electronic drums to your service, don't put them on a riser for all to see. Place them in a part of the worship space that is less obvious. Instead of adding a full drum kit to the worship music, consider adding a single percussive instrument on a schedule similar to the one above. If you're planning to add electric guitar, don't use the distortion or crunch channel on the amp, as this is the sound most closely associated with rock and roll. Instead, use a clean sound, possibly with a touch of chorus or reverb. Keep the volume low, and keep the musical parts very sparse. Overplaying on any new instrument will be counterproductive as it draws attention to itself. Keeping change below the radar gives people the opportunity to acclimate to the new instruments over time instead of having it thrust in their face!

- *Don't talk about it too much:* One of the biggest mistakes churches make when integrating something new into their worship is talking about it too much beforehand. Preparing your congregation for change is vitally important. But some churches build expectations to the point that the new element in the service becomes the focal point of everyone's attention. This is the opposite of the *transparency* that we're after. I encourage churches to prepare their congregation in a general, non-specific way. Then slowly and subtly introduce the new instrument. After the instrument has been introduced, *then* it's okay to talk about it. In other words, instead of pumping people full of expectations, or even fear, let them experience the benefits of music technology used appropriately. Then tell them what they've just experienced.

- *Do it well:* The only compelling argument I've ever heard against adding music technology to a traditional service is when the resistance stems from the fact that the music was executed poorly. In the midst of change, it's hard for people to separate the baby from the bath water. Therefore make every effort to be as prepared as possible. If you're introducing new instruments slowly, you'll have more time to prepare. Lead with strength. Use your best musicians. Don't give those resistant to change an excuse to grumble.

Vince Parks is executive director of Ministry at Gloria Dei Lutheran Church in Houston, Texas. In addition to Vince's staff leadership role, he's also an organist at the church. Gloria Dei has a digital organ that uses sampling technology to emulate the sound of a pipe organ. In addition to its own capabilities, the organ also has MIDI capability. Although Vince specializes in traditional church music, he has been quick to see the value that MIDI technology can bring his music ministry. Through using the organ's built-in sequencer, Vince is able to hear himself play anywhere in Gloria Dei's sanctuary.

"The best place to listen to the organ is not always at the console," Vince says. Vince uses the MIDI sequencing capability as a practice tool, allowing him to record and play back his own performances.

Speaking of stops, or sounds an organ can make, Vince states, "Organists always want something that they don't have. MIDI has become the answer." Vince frequently uses the MIDI output of the organ to play an external sound module. He's found that mixing traditional and non-traditional organ sounds can add a great deal to the worship service. Vince tends to gravitate toward patches such as string ensembles and pads, or solo patches, like an oboe or clarinet.

***

The key to success in using music technology in a traditional church setting is to remember our focus. We need to honor heritage even as we look forward to the future. We need to engage people, not distract them. And, finally, we need to move slowly and subtly as we introduce new elements to the service—all the while embracing excellence in ministry.

A sound module can be used to enhance a traditional instrument, or it can give a modern instrument a big dose of heritage. By adding a Roland VK-8M Organ Sound Module to any MIDI keyboard, you can create the timeless sound of a classic tonewheel organ with all the performance features, including drawbars and rotary speaker.

TWELVE

ADVANCED APPLICATIONS FOR MUSIC TECHNOLOGY IN WORSHIP

This book is primarily a guided tour through the world of music technology in worship. Thus far, we've placed our focus on the most commonly used applications for music technology. However, there are some new and advanced technologies that are just now beginning to find their way into the hands of church musicians. This chapter is dedicated to some emerging technologies that hold great promise for the future of music technology in worship. They include:

- Virtual instruments
- Using loops in the context of worship
- Creating a worship recording

Virtual Instruments

We've already established that keyboard synthesizers are very much like little computers with piano keys. We've also discovered that some synthesizers don't have piano keys at all. Some are *sound modules*, while others are *guitar synthesizers* or even *electronic drum kits*. Building on this concept is the emerging world of *virtual instruments*. As the name suggests, a *virtual instrument* is not an object at all. Rather, it's a piece of software that, when coupled with the right computer, functions as a musical instrument. Today's computer processors are so powerful that they have become great hosts for *virtual instruments*. This is made possible not only by the computer's horsepower but by the ability to communicate MIDI information to and from the computer quickly and easily. Let's break this down a bit.

To physically play a virtual instrument, you'll need five components:

- *Computer:* As far as the computer goes, requirements differ depending on which virtual instrument is being used. This information is readily available on the software packaging or on the software-manufacturer's website. But the bottom line is this: A computer with a fast processor and lots of RAM will give you better performance.

- *MIDI interface:* Just about any MIDI interface will do. The key is finding an interface that best accommodates (has enough inputs and outputs) all of your MIDI devices.

- *MIDI controller:* Any device that can send MIDI information (such as a keyboard or guitar synthesizer) will do. In other words, anything with a MIDI OUT port.

- *Audio interface:* This is the same type of audio interface used in a hard disk recording setup. Using a high-quality audio interface will improve sound quality and help eliminate latency issues. Many audio interfaces serve as a MIDI interface as well.

- *Virtual instrument software:* Although still an emerging technology, there are already a variety of virtual instruments available.

Atmosphere, from Spectrasonics, is a virtual instrument containing over three gigabytes of synthesizer string and pad samples. It can function as a stand-alone program, and is compatible with a number of plug-in formats, including VST, RTAS, and MAS.

Although some are designed to be stand-alone applications, most virtual instruments come in the form of software *plug-ins*, which require a sequencing/digital audio recording program in which to run. VST, AU, DXi, RTAS, and MAS are examples of commonly used plug-in formats. Check your sequencing/digital audio recording software's documentation to see which formats are supported.

Some virtual instruments utilize sample-based technology while others use *modeling* technology to create their sounds. Sample-based software applications generally come with large sample libraries (some as large as three gigabytes or more) that need to be installed on the computer's hard drive. Obviously, you'll want to make sure that you have enough room for these files. Some sample-based virtual instruments also provide the ability to import third-party sample libraries. Many sample libraries are available in several file formats. Your software documentation will let you know which sample formats (if any) are compatible.

Let's take a look at a typical *virtual instrument* setup:

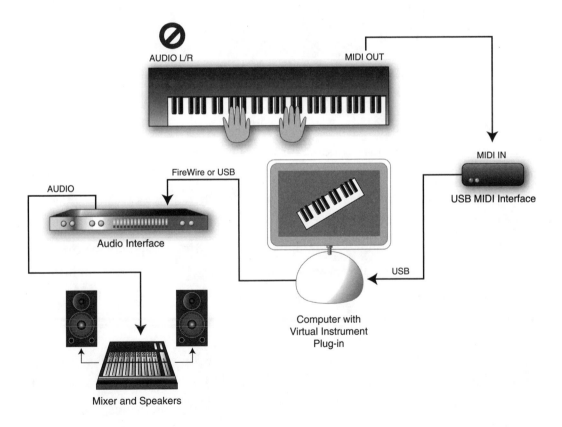

In most software applications, a virtual instrument is accessed by *inserting* the instrument plug-in on an audio channel. The audio output of that channel would be routed to one or more outputs on the audio interface. The audio channel in the software would also be configured to receive MIDI information on a particular MIDI channel. When the keyboard is played, MIDI note information is sent via a MIDI cable to the MIDI interface, which is connected to the computer via a USB cable. The virtual instrument software on the computer reads the incoming MIDI note information and plays a sound. This audio, created by the virtual instrument or *software synthesizer*, is sent to the audio interface. The sound of the virtual instrument is heard from the audio outputs of the audio interface. It's important to note that, in our example, *no sound is coming from the keyboard itself—it's just a MIDI controller*!

Given the fact that these instruments are easily customized and relatively inexpensive, virtual instruments are likely to be at the top of many church musicians' wish lists. It may not be long before keyboard players, armed only with a MIDI controller and a laptop computer, become commonplace in worship. However, the ultimate value of virtual instruments is not found in replacing keyboards or sound modules. Rather, the emergence of virtual-instrument technology adds yet another color to the church musician's palette.

Using "Loops" in a Worship Context

A *loop* is a short phrase of music that is repeated in such a way that it provides a rhythmic and sometimes harmonic motif, establishing the *feel* of a song. Although loops were originally a niche production technique used in a very narrow range of music, loops of various kinds can now be found across the spectrum of contemporary music styles. Many churches are finding that loops can enhance worship, providing an air of familiarity and relevance to the music. Most loops are very short—usually a measure or two. Some loops contain only percussive sounds, leaving the harmony for the live instruments. And while it might seem redundant to use a percussive *drum loop* in addition to live drums, this complex rhythmic sound is precisely what many musicians are after when using loops.

It's important to note that the term loop refers to how the phrase is *used* and not how it is *created*. In other words, a loop could be a MIDI sequence or a piece of digital audio that is repeated. Because most loops are brief, creating loops is not difficult; in fact, it's pretty easy. Think of it as a two-measure song. Creating a MIDI loop is as simple as creating a two-measure sequence. Creating an audio loop is as easy as creating a two-measure hard disk recording. Loops can be created on virtually any software or hardware sequencer or hard disk recorder. There are even a few software and hardware tools that specialize in creating and playing loops.

While creating a loop is not difficult at all, *using* that loop in a worship context can be a bit tricky. Because a loop (sequenced or recorded) is essentially *fixed* in terms of tempo, it's vitally important that the other musicians are able to follow it easily. This is a new experience for many instrumentalists who are used to a level of flexibility in terms of tempo. A loop can quickly deteriorate into a "train wreck" if the loop and the band get out of sync! Obviously, this defeats the whole purpose of using a loop in the first place. The key to using loops successfully is found in addressing the following:

- *How does the song begin?* Sometimes it may be desirable to begin a song with one or two measures of the loop as a count-off for the instrumentalists. This can work well, but only if the loop is rhythmic enough to provide an adequate tempo reference for the musicians. If you want the instruments and the loop to begin playing together, you'll need to create a click track that is only audible to one or more instrumentalists. This is usually accomplished by providing a click track to the drummer (or conductor, if present) through headphones. This way the drummer or conductor can cue the rest of the ensemble with a quiet count-off without the congregation having to hear the click track.

- *How long is the song?* It may be possible to predetermine the precise number of measures in a worship song. If so, a loop can be created to start and stop at specific points. Some worship leaders prefer an open-ended approach to worship music and would find such preprogramming limiting. For those who prefer a bit more freedom or spontaneity in worship, a loop can be cued to start or stop manually as well. The trick here is finding a way to start and stop the loop quickly and easily.

- *Do we need a click track?* A rhythmically oriented loop may provide enough of a tempo reference to preempt the need for a click track. However, a click track is needed if a silent count-off is desired. Sometimes, a loop is programmed to play on the chorus of a song, but not on the verse. In this case, a click track is needed throughout the song in order for the band to stay in sync with the loop. Because a click track is just for the musicians, it's important to find a way to keep it inaudible to the congregation. Again, this is usually accomplished by feeding the click to headphones worn by the drummer (and conductor, if present). If the drummer plays to the click, and the rest of the ensemble plays to the drummer, then everyone should stay in sync.

It's highly advantageous to play with a loop in rehearsal before trying it in worship. In fact, it's a good idea to introduce this concept to your musicians in a rehearsal long before you ever try it live. Even if you don't have a due date for using a loop in worship, try it with your team in a non-threatening environment. Since your drummer is likely to be the person primarily responsible for staying in sync with the loop, give him or her some time in advance to practice. Many drummers have never practiced with a metronome, much less a loop, and may find it very challenging to stay in tempo with a loop. Therefore, don't put your drummer on the spot in front of the band until he or she is comfortable with it.

This philosophy holds true regarding any kind of new technology you're bringing to the table: People first. Set your team members up to succeed. If your team is behind the idea, you have a much better chance of the congregation embracing it as well.

- *Format*: How will the loop be played during worship? From a computer sequencer? From a stand-alone hard disk recorder? From a CD player? Each of these solutions are common ways of playing loops. It's important to find the one that best fits your own needs.

Creating and using a click track: Most sequencers and hard disk recorders contain the ability to automatically create a click track. If a loop is being played directly from the sequencer or hard disk recorder, the solution is fairly straight-forward: Assign the click sound to a separate output channel on the synthesizer or hard disk recorder. Run that channel through a separate input on the mixing board. Route the signal to the headphones of anyone who needs to hear the click.

Some churches prefer to play loops from CD. Although it's possible that the loop originally came from a MIDI sequence, at some point the sequence would have to be recorded to hard disk (as digital audio) in order to burn it to CD. When using a loop that is on a CD, the click track (if necessary) is recorded on one side of the stereo spectrum (i.e., left) and the loop is recorded on the other (i.e., right). This allows the two signals (loop and click) to be separated and routed to two different channels on the mixing board. The loop is routed to the speakers, while the click is routed only to the headphones. While this method adds an extra step to the process, it provides a very convenient way to use loops in a worship setting.

CHAPTER TWELVE: ADVANCED APPLICATIONS FOR MUSIC TECHNOLOGY IN WORSHIP

Creating a Worship Recording

As high-quality recording technology has become more affordable and easier to use, an increasing number of churches have begun creating worship recordings for their congregation and community. MIDI sequencing, hard disk recording, and CD-burning technology have enabled churches of all sizes to produce recordings that would have been unthinkable only a few years ago! While full-length live worship recordings have become commonplace, churches are beginning to use worship recordings in new and creative ways. They include:

- *Edification:* Putting worship music in the hands of your congregation allows them to experience worship in a powerful and personal way during everyday tasks such as commuting and exercise, or while studying or praying.

- *Preparation:* Your vocal team, choir, and instrumentalists will benefit from custom rehearsal CDs. You can also use hard disk recorders to empower leaders in your ministry and leverage your time as we discussed in Chapter Nine.

- *Teaching new material:* A recording is a great way to introduce a congregation to new worship music. This way, when a song is first introduced in the worship service, the congregation is empowered to sing with familiarity and confidence, thus enhancing the worship experience.

- *Promotional:* Promote your church, ministry, or event by giving out free copies of your worship music.

- *Fundraising:* Use your recording to raise funds for various ministry events. For example, let your junior high kids send themselves to camp by creating a custom recording and selling it to friends and relatives.

A custom worship recording provides the congregation with something unique to celebrate. It can provide encouragement and hope and reinforce the value for worship in our everyday lives.

As we learned in Chapter Nine, hard disk recording is becoming increasingly more affordable and easy to use. Does this mean that creating a worship recording is an easy endeavor? *Yes... and no.* Capturing sound on disk is the easy part. But creating a great-sounding recording can be tricky business and is a subject that could fill the pages of an entire book. Nevertheless, in the remaining space of this chapter, we'll examine some helpful hints for producing great-sounding worship recordings.

Recording Strategy

One of the first things to do is to create a recording strategy. Will this be a *live* recording where all the instruments and vocals are recorded at once? Or will each part be added incrementally? The answers to these questions are not only related to personal preference, they will dictate what equipment is needed, what facilities will be necessary, what options you'll have during recording and mixing, and how long the recording project will take—to name a few.

Creating a live recording is a great way to capture a worship experience. Each instrumentalist and vocalist is experiencing the same music at the same time. As a result, it's very likely that the *feel* of the recording will be a good one. Recording everything at once also saves time, and possibly money if any outside contractors (musicians or sound engineers) are being used. A live recording is very demanding technically as the recording equipment needs to be able to handle a large number of tracks at once. It's true that various parts of the ensemble can be *sub-mixed* in order to limit the number of tracks. But doing so limits the mixing process and the ability to fix mistakes after the fact. For example, if drums, bass, guitar, and keyboard are sub-mixed to a stereo mix (two tracks), any mistakes made by a single instrument would require all four instrumentalists to re-track their parts. On the other hand, recording each instrument to a different track would require a large number of inputs on the recorder. While there are some great solutions to this dilemma, many hard disk recording devices allow only eight inputs at once. Therefore, a recorder capable of recording large numbers of tracks at once is highly recommended for a live recording situation.

Creating a recording where each part is added incrementally is far less demanding technically. A quality recording can be made with a fairly modest hard disk recorder. When creating such a recording, it's important to map out how and when each part will be recorded. For example, vocals would not usually be recorded first. Without an accompaniment track, the singers would have nothing to sing to. Rather, it's best to start with the instrumental tracks. It is, however, okay to record vocals with a basic accompaniment

First, you record a guitar.

▶ Track 1

While listening to the guitar play back, you record a vocal.

▶ Track 1

▶ Track 2

And so on...

▶ Track 1

▶ Track 2

▶ Track 3

The overdubbing process

instrument first, adding other tracks later. A more common track order would be to first record drums, bass, and perhaps one additional instrument (such as keyboards or guitar). Then any other instruments would add their parts one at a time. This process is called *overdubbing*. When the song is nearing completion, the vocalists would add their parts. This method provides a great deal of flexibility when recording, as each part can be recorded and edited separately in order to ensure musical excellence. However, it's also a much slower process.

Conserving Tracks

Because some hard disk recorders are limited in the number of tracks they can record or play back, it's important to learn how to keep the track count down. One great track-saving tip is to use electronic drums, such as the Roland V-Drums, instead of acoustic drums. Most acoustic drum kits are large enough to utilize eight microphones, which feed eight tracks while recording. Using electronic drums can reduce that number to two. Because electronic drums can be *mixed* inside of the percussion sound module, only a stereo mix (two tracks) is needed. Another track-saving trick is to record a vocal team with two microphones instead of having individual microphones for each singer.

Don't Overuse Effects

The digital effects included with most hard disk recorders are wonderful tools. They can add a sense of depth to a recording, enabling it to come alive as we listen. But they can also be overused. The temptation for those new to recording is to use effects *because they can*. While it's fun to hear the music change when we add an effect, we may not even realize that all we're doing is creating a distraction or muddying the sound. Here's a great rule of thumb for those new to effects: When adding any effect, increase the volume until the effect is audible. Then back it off just a bit. Subtlety is the key!

Consult a Pro

Consider bringing in a *ringer* to help get you started. If your goal is to create a recording that compares favorably to commercially available recordings, you need to learn how those recordings are made. Recording engineering is an art unto itself and cannot be learned in a matter of days or weeks. While bringing in an engineer may require a modest investment, the result will be well worth it. If you choose wisely, you'll not only get a great-sounding recording, but you'll learn a lot in the process as well. Plus, if you're using a hard disk recording system that was purchased by you or the church, the money you'll save in studio time alone will more than pay for a professional engineer or producer.

Don't Forget the Rules

When tackling a project as exciting as recording a CD, it's easy to forget some important musical principles. Each instrument is still bound by the same guidelines that we explored earlier. The *100 Percent Rule* still applies. Keyboard players still need to be wary of stepping on the bass player's turf. And guitar players need to choose their sounds wisely (and musically). In a worship service, if these rules are violated, the moment comes and goes. But on a recording, musical train wrecks are preserved for posterity. That's not a legacy that most of us would aspire to.

So go forth and be musical!

THIRTEEN

PURCHASING EQUIPMENT FOR YOUR ORGANIZATION

In this book, we've explored a vast landscape of musical instrument technologies. New instruments bring a level of excitement with them, so the process of purchasing them shouldn't rob your joy. In this chapter, we'll look at some helpful tips for making regret-free purchasing decisions.

Identify Your Needs

In Chapter Five, we discussed the importance of prioritizing your needs before purchasing a keyboard. The same is true for any electronic musical instrument. It's easy to be seduced by some of the fancy features that come with today's equipment. It doesn't matter how great the screen on your keyboard looks if it cannot create the kind of music you need! Make a list. Check it twice (sorry, I couldn't resist). Keep your list with you during your search process.

Do Your Homework

Just as in school, there's no way around this. If you educate yourself, you'll greatly increase the likelihood of making a wise choice. How do you get educated? Read everything you can. The Internet is a great resource. There are some great books and periodicals that can help you as well. The Next Step Resource Guide in the Appendix will get you started.

Play Everything Under the Sun

If you're new to electronic musical instruments, you may find it tough to make that priority list of needs. Throughout the process, it's helpful to audition every instrument that you can get your hands on. It will assist you in developing your preferences, which will shape your list of needs. Don't make a purchase as important as this a one-step process. Most churches want to see their instrument investments last for more than a couple of years. Making the appropriate time commitment in the search process will ensure that your investment will remain useful as long as possible.

Find Some Comrades

There's nothing more valuable than knowledgeable people in the search process. Find people with the same general needs as your congregation. This may involve contacting churches in your community or denomination. Most church musicians will be happy to share their experiences with you. Many will even let you try their instruments. Although people often have biases toward certain equipment, it's still an invaluable part of the process to see how others have solved similar needs.

Kent Morris is an audio/video systems designer for Cornerstone Media. He also teaches at various workshops and writes technology-related articles for publications such as *Worship Leader* magazine. Kent has also been a pastor, a live sound engineer, a studio owner, and even a musician on the worship team. Because of the many hats he has worn, Kent has a unique perspective when advising church leaders on prospective equipment purchases.

"Good music store owners and managers live vicariously through their best customers," Kent says. "Many of them are musicians or were at one time. They want to see you succeed!"

Kent believes this is precisely why a strong relationship with a dealer is invaluable. Kent also encourages church musicians to seek out musicians from other churches in their area. He believes that a strong fellowship among musicians will facilitate an environment of learning and inevitably result in wise purchasing decisions.

Develop a Relationship with a Dealer

When searching for new equipment, churches commonly look for a dealer (music store) with a great selection and perhaps, more importantly, low prices. But we don't want to be shortsighted in this process. I encourage church leaders to make every effort to develop a relationship with a local dealer. Most musical instrument dealers are genuinely interested in meeting your needs with practical solutions that fit your budget. Developing a relationship over time will allow a dealer to address your needs more effectively. A church that has a strong relationship with a dealer may find that they're able to try equipment in a service before buying it. Many dealers will offer inexpensive rental of additional equipment for special events. In some cases, a relationship with a local dealer is not possible due to geographic or other reasons. There are some very good mail-order dealers that can ship a wide variety of products just about anywhere within days. But whether the dealer is local or national, the bottom line is that a healthy relationship with a dealer provides you and your congregation with an advocate.

The Golden Rule

In our quest for the best deal, it's important to be a good witness. Yes, we have to be good stewards of our resources, but dealers need to make a profit to meet their obligations. While I wouldn't suggest that we pay more than a fair price, we need to realize that it's in our best interest for a dealer to stay in business over the long haul. We need to be aware of the message we are communicating, as well as the consequences of negotiating that extra dollar off the price. We may have saved a buck, but we, in the process, could have lost an advocate. The best price isn't always the best deal.

FOURTEEN

KEEPING THE MAIN THING, THE MAIN THING

As we come to the end of our journey through the world of music technology in worship, let's take a quick glance at our travels. We began by exploring the past and how it has shaped our present. We discovered that music technology is no longer the exclusive domain of keyboard players and is available to a wide variety of instruments. We learned how technology can save us time and empower us to create music that was previously beyond our reach.

An underlying theme runs through it all, which has remained unstated until now: Music technology, impressive as it may be, is ultimately a supportive ministry tool that is only truly effective when it is used to enhance the worship life of a congregation. While this sentiment is easily agreed upon, achieving this goal week after week is another story. In real-life ministry, it's easy to get so immersed in technical possibility that we lose sight of what we're ultimately after. When we cross that line, technology can become what drives our service planning, our rehearsals, and, eventually, our worship services. So how do we keep the *main thing, the main thing?*

"Technology adds more colors to our palette," says Ian Cron, senior pastor of Trinity Church in Greenwich, Connecticut. "It provides us with the ability to create a sensory experience of God."

When it comes to approaching technology in worship, Ian's perspective is somewhat unique in that he's both a senior pastor and an accomplished professional musician. Although Trinity Church is well known in their community as a church with a high value for the arts, Ian is well aware that with the incredible potential that technology brings, also comes the ability to undermine core ministry values.

"Technology can become its own god by drawing attention to itself in worship," Ian says. He encourages church leaders to possess a clear vision of what worship is in their congregation. "It can't be driven by fad or by the availability of technology."

Central to Ian's convictions is the value that technology should always be subordinate to people and ministry values. "The Gospel is a very fleshy thing," Ian says. "There always has to be a human-touch factor in worship."

"How you use technology should grow out of who you are and what you're trying to do," states Dave Miller, worship pastor at Lakeland Community Church in Holland, Michigan.

While Dave shares Ian's concern that technology unchecked can eclipse our ministry values, he also points out how music technology has brought his team together. "Being able to get an original hard disk recording to our band quickly has enabled our rehearsals to become more collaborative," Dave says. "When our pastor decides on a direction for his message on Monday, we can create an original recording ready for distribution on Tuesday or Wednesday." When the band members have a chance to learn the music *before* rehearsal, they're able to create better music. "It allows us to get past the same old three-chord arrangements," says Dave.

While these two church leaders have never met, and their churches are over a thousand miles apart, they share a common conviction that ministry values should drive how we approach technology. When this conviction is put into practice consistently, music technology can help unleash the arts in a very powerful way in our congregations. This core value for keeping the main thing, the main thing works across denominational lines, in churches traditional and contemporary, large and small.

Finally, I'd like to share a bit of my own experience. I've served on the staff of a mega-church and two church plants. In my coaching ministry, I've served churches of less than fifty and a church of over 15,000. I've worked with traditional liturgical churches and cutting-edge contemporary churches representing over a dozen denominations. Over the years I've heard literally hundreds of stories from worship leaders describing the joys and failures of integrating music technology into their ministries. While I make no claims of originality in my conviction, I've found that there are two seemingly opposite, yet inseparable values that need to be in place in order to keep worship at the center of performance:

- *The vertical aspect of worship:* Let us not forget the object of our worship. When we begin to lose the *vertical* emphasis in our worship, we become prone to self-promotion and, ultimately, let our own desires or the desires of others shape our ministry. Our worship is essentially a reflection of *who* God is. While our theology may differ, we can undoubtedly agree that God loves us and is continually seeking a relationship with us. Music has historically played a very special role in painting this picture of God. If we can embrace the vertical aspect of worship, we can begin to explore what music technology can bring to the worship experience.

- *The horizontal aspect of worship:* Often overlooked in our self-obsessed culture, corporate worship is designed to be just that: corporate. Worship has historically been inseparable from the concept of community. True community in worship can only be found in a proper understanding of the *vertical* and *horizontal* relationships that exist in worship. One of the great dangers in bringing technology into worship is that under the guise of excellence, we end up replacing people. While we need to steward the gifts we've been given (both individually and corporately) to the best of our abilities, we must make sure not to take our eyes off the horizontal aspect of worship, which is manifested in community.

So, produce a worship CD using hard disk recording. But do so to celebrate community in your congregation. *Create a MIDI sequence.* But do so to enhance the vertical aspect of worship or to help your worship team members grow. *Learn all you can about technology.* But don't let your learning time displace your time with God and people. *Get excited about all that music technology can bring to your ministry.* But don't lose site of He who brings us all good things. Remain committed to your worship values, and you'll see how these amazingly powerful tools will change your congregation's worship life for the better!

> *I would gladly see all arts, especially music, in the service of Him who has given and created them.*
>
> —Martin Luther

APPENDIX: NEXT STEPS

Our journey through the world of music technology in worship has been a mile wide and a foot deep. Though some of the concepts we've explored may be new to you, we've really only scratched the surface of what these amazing instruments can do. So where do you get more information? This journey would not be complete without identifying some next steps for future exploration.

Books and Periodicals

There are some great books that have been written on many of the topics we've covered. There are also some great music technology magazines. Most of these periodicals include coverage of emerging technologies, new equipment reviews, and even regular columns dedicated to those just starting out. There is a resource guide at the end of this chapter that includes a few book and periodical selections.

Web Resources

There are a lot of great (and not so great) resources for further music technology exploration available on the Internet. Manufacturer's websites are a great place to learn about equipment. Also, some music technology magazines have their own websites with archived articles and even interactive message boards. There are even websites dedicated to reviewing musical equipment. But, remember, there is a lot of bad information on the Internet as well. Be careful to confirm the information you receive by checking with a dealer or the manufacturer. New sites are popping up all the time. Use an Internet search engine to find the instrument category you're looking for. We've included a good number of sites in the Resource Guide on page 155.

Training Materials

More and more, companies are releasing training materials that supplement the owner's manual. Some manufacturers have video resources available to coach you through learning an instrument. There are also third-party resources available—especially in the area of music software. Some are even in the form of interactive CD-ROMs or DVDs for the computer. These resources are becoming more common and are a great way to learn a particular instrument, software application, or aspect of music technology.

Roland has created a number of video owners manuals to help demonstrate the operation of popular products.

Workshops

Perhaps the quickest way to jump-start your learning process is to spend time with an expert. The easiest (and least expensive) way to do this is to attend a workshop. There are workshops available at music stores as well as colleges and universities. In recent years, organizations like Maranatha Music and Integrity Music have offered helpful workshops that include music-technology classes. Some large churches are even offering training in this area. Check the resource guide for more info.

Custom Coaching

As someone who provides coaching to churches, I have to admit this is my favorite. One of the reasons that I wanted to provide this kind of service is because I've had some people *build into me* in similar settings. I find that I learn best in this kind of environment. To this day, I seek out coaches who can bring me up to speed on anything from playing a new musical style to learning a new technology. Truth be told, I received a fair amount of coaching during the writing of this book! Customized instruction is likely to be the most expensive option for continued education. But, if you're like me, you may find that an hour or two with an expert saves another valuable commodity: time.

Next Steps Resource Guide

This is not an exhaustive list or an endorsement. Rather, this list is designed to provide helpful examples of the types of resources that are available. In other words, we may have missed some good ones. So keep your eyes peeled.

Books:

- *All About Hard Disk Recording* by Robby Berman
- *All About Electronic Drums* by Mike Snyder
- *Keyboard Wisdom* by Steve Goomas
- *The Heart of the Artist* by Rory Noland
- *How MIDI Works* by Peter Alexander
- *MIDI for Musicians* by Craig Anderton
- *The MIDI Manual* by David Miles Huber
- *The MIDI Companion* by Jeffrey Rona
- *All About Music Technology in Worship* by Steve Young

Periodicals:

- *Christian Musician*—www.christianmusician.com
- *Bass Player*—www.bassplayer.com
- *Church Production*—www.churchproduction.com
- *Church Sound & Song*—www.soundandsong.com
- *Electronic Musician*—www.electronicmusician.com
- *EQ*—www.eqmag.com
- *Guitar Player*—www.guitarplayer.com
- *Home Recording*—www.homerecordingmag.com
- *Keyboard*—www.keyboardmag.com
- *MIDI in Ministry*—www.rolandus.com
- *Mix*—www.mixonline.com
- *Modern Drummer*—www.moderndrummer.com
- *Recording*—www.recordingmag.com
- *Sound on Sound*—www.soundonsound.com
- *Technologies for Worship*—www.tfwm.com
- *Worship Leader*—www.worshipleader.com
- *Worship Magazine*—www.worshipmagazine.com

Instructional Videos:

- Carl Albrecht (drums)　　　*available at* www.worshipmusic.com
- Paul Baloche (guitar)　　　*available at* www.leadworship.com
- Ed Kerr (keyboards)　　　*available at* www.kerrtunes.com
- Norm Stockton (bass)　　　*available at* www.normstockton.com
- Tommy Walker (guitar)　　　*available at* www.getdownrecords.com
- Creative Guitar Techniques　*available at* www.worshipmusic.com

Web:

Hardware Manufacturers:

www.akg.com

www.alesis.com

www.apple.com

www.aviom.com

www.behringer.com

www.bossus.com

www.brianmooreguitars.com

www.crateamps.com

www.clavia.se

www.digitech.com

www.dod.com

www.edirol.com

www.elixirstrings.com

www.emu.com

www.fender.com

www.fostex.com

www.gibson.com

www.jblpro.com

www.kawaius.com

www.korg.com

www.kurzweilmusicsystems.com

www.lexicon.com

www.line6.com

www.mackie.com

www.marshallamps.com

www.martinguitar.com

www.m-audio.com

www.monstercable.com

www.motu.com

www.onstagestands.com

www.peavey.com

www.rolandus.com

www.samsontech.com

www.sennheiserusa.com

www.shure.com

www.skbcases.com

www.tascam.com

www.taylorguitars.com

www.tcelectronic.com

www.ultimatesupport.com

www.voxamps.co.uk

www.yamaha.com

www.zoom.co.jp

Software Manufacturers:

www.ableton.com (Live)

www.antarestech.com (Auto-Tune)

www.apple.com (iTunes, GarageBand)

www.bigfishaudio.com (sampler libraries)

www.bitheadz.com (Unity)

www.cakewalk.com (Cakewalk/Sonar)

www.digidesign.com (Pro Tools)

www.drumsforyou.com (custom drum trax)

www.emagic.de (Logic)

www.ikmultimedia.com (effect plug-ins)

www.ilio.com (sampler libraries)

www.makemusic.com (Finale)

www.massenburg.com (effect plug-ins)

www.mcdsp.com (effect plug-ins)

www.motu.com (Digital Performer)

www.nativeinstruments.de (B4)

www.pgmusic.com (PowerTracks)

www.propellerheads.se (Reason)

www.sampleheads.com (sample libraries)

www.sibelius.com (Sibelius)

www.soundforge.com (ACID)

www.spectrasonics.net (Stylus, Atmosphere)

www.steinberg.net (Cubase)

www.tascamgiga.com (GigaStudio)

www.uaudio.com (effect plug-ins)

www.waves.com (effect plug-ins)

Training, Forums, and Users Groups:

www.artsimpact.com

www.audiblefaith.com

www.ccli.com

www.churchsoundcheck.com

www.crosswalk.com

www.digitalmusicdoctor.com

www.fantomized.info

www.musicplayer.com

www.prosoundweb.com

www.soundonsound.com

www.vdrums.com

www.vsplanet.com

www.worshipconnection.org

www.worshiptech.com

www.worshiptogether.com

Workshops & Conferences:

- Calvary Chapel—www.calvarychapelmusic.com
- Christian Musician Summit—www.christianmusiciansummit.com
- Hillsongs—www.hillsong.com
- Integrity Music—www.seminars4worship.com
- Maranatha Music—www.worshipleaderworkshop.com
- Purpose Driven—www.purposedriven.com
- Soul Survivor—www.soulsurvivorusa.com
- Willow Creek Association—www.willowcreek.com
- Worship Institute—www.worshipinstitute.com
- Worship Together—www.worshiptogether.com
- Gospel Music Association—www.gospelmusic.com

INDEX

About the Author

Steve Young is the director of creative arts at Renaissance Church in Millburn, NJ. He is also the founder of Arts Impact, a creative coaching ministry that serves churches in the area of worship and the arts. Steve has partnered with organizations such as the Willow Creek Association, Maranatha Music, Roland Corporation U.S., and Concordia University Irvine, as well as churches of various sizes and denominations nationally. He has performed and recorded with various Christian artists and remains active as a keyboard player, arranger, and producer in the New York City area. Steve lives in Short Hills, New Jersey, with his wife Victoria, and their two young boys, Jordan and Brady.

Steve can be contacted through his website: www.artsimpact.com